Julia Gillian

(and the Dream of the Dog)

by **Alison McGhee**

with pictures by
Drazen Kozjan

SCHOLASTIC PRESS   NEW YORK

LIBRARY OF CONGRESS CATALOGING-IN-PUBLICATION DATA

McGhee, Alison, 1960 –
Julia Gillian (and the dream of the dog) / by Alison McGhee ;
illustrated by Drazen Kozjan. — 1st ed.   p.   cm.
Summary: While trying to cope with more school work, including an assignment in her least favorite subject, reading, a sixth-grade girl faces her toughest challenge as her beloved dog — and lifelong companion — nears the end of his life.

ISBN 978-0-545-03351-0

[1. Dogs — Fiction.   2. Death — Fiction.   3. Reading — Fiction.
4. Middle schools — Fiction.   5. Schools — Fiction.]   I. Kozjan, Drazen, ill.   II. Title.
PZ7.M4784675Jun 2010   [Fic] — dc22   2009027129

10   9   8   7   6   5   4   3   2   1   10   11   12   13   14

Printed in the U.S.A.   23
First edition, July 2010

ACKNOWLEDGMENTS

My thanks to the wonderful and talented Tracy Mack, Emellia Zamani, Holly McGhee, and Kara LaReau, each of whom helped shepherd this book into being, and thanks also to Marijka Kostiw for her expertise in book design. Thanks to Drazen Kozjan, whose talent brought Julia Gillian and Bigfoot to life (and let me see what they looked like). Finally, thanks and love to Brad Zellar, whose great and tender love for his dogs is an inspiration.

CHAPTER ONE
Shall We?

"Welcome to sixth grade," said Mr. Lamonte. "We have a great many forms to fill out, so let's get started, shall we?"

Julia Gillian exchanged a look with her best friend, Bonwit Keller. Mr. Lamonte, their homeroom teacher, was famous at Lake Harriet School for this particular phrase. Each year, until the new batch of sixth-graders had grown used to hearing it, "shall we?" rose from the hallways, lunchroom, and playground nearly any time of day. It was an irresistible phrase.

Mr. Lamonte began making the rounds of the room, depositing a packet of forms on each student's desk: *Thunk. Thunk. Thunk.*

I

"Please, students," said Mr. Lamonte. "Let us try to get these back tomorrow, shall we?"

How Julia Gillian wanted to say *shall we?* in just the way that Mr. Lamonte said it, with the dip in the *shall* and the upswing in the *we*, but she resisted. *Thunk.* She stared down at the batch of forms that he had just dropped onto her desk.

Each new school year brought the same forms, all of which needed to be filled out, signed, and returned immediately. Julia Gillian, under the influence of her schoolteacher parents, always returned her forms the very next day. So did Bonwit, who was conscientious by nature. Their friend Cerise Cronin generally had hers back within a week, while others, such as Lathrop Fallon, sometimes straggled their way into October. This was a terrible thing, because extreme stragglers were not allowed to go on field trips.

Two years ago, in fact, Lathrop had once been forced to sit in the lunchroom all day, doing extra homework, while everyone else was at the Oliver Kelley Living History Farm harvesting vegetables, making applesauce, and forking hay into the hay barn for the long winter to come.

"Take them home," said Mr. Lamonte, who had *thunk*ed the last packet of forms onto the last desk. "Go through them with your parent or legal guardian. Sign where necessary. And then bring them back. Let's be prompt, shall we?"

A whispered "shall we?" rose from three distinct places in the classroom, including Cerise's desk. The defenses were already beginning to crumble. Julia Gillian resisted.

"You are sixth-graders now," said Mr. Lamonte. "And as such, you are middle schoolers."

He leaned back against his desk, crossed his arms, raised one eyebrow, and scanned the room slowly, nodding as he did, a habit known school-wide as the Lamonte Look.

"As of right now," he said, "your lives are fundamentally altered."

Julia Gillian wasn't sure she liked the sound of that. She was quite happy with her life just as it was. After all, she loved her parents, her friends, her school, and her dog, Bigfoot. She liked the routine of her daily life — her long walks with Bigfoot, weekend days doing art projects with Bonwit, visits with her downstairs neighbors Zap and Enzo, making papier-mâché masks to add to her collection, Saturday night dinners with her parents at the Quang Vietnamese Restaurant. She looked over at Bonwit, who was picking at his thumbnail, which was something he did when nervous.

"No longer are you one-classroom, one-teacher students," continued Mr. Lamonte. "No longer are you the oldest elementary students. Instead, you are the youngest middle schoolers."

Mr. Lamonte uncrossed his arms and swept the room with another Lamonte Look.

"I believe the term is *Sixlet*," he said. "Not that we teachers would use such a term."

The students were silent. *Sixlet* was indeed the term for sixth-graders, just as *Sevvies* and *Crazy Eights* referred to the seventh- and eighth-graders, but teachers weren't supposed to know those nicknames.

"Let me introduce you to a concept that will help you navigate the sometimes tricky waters of sixth grade," said Mr. Lamonte. "In order to accomplish a task, keep focused on the task itself. Rule out all the factors that might adversely affect the outcome. We call this process controlling for variables."

Bonwit and Julia Gillian looked at each other. They didn't really understand what Mr. Lamonte was talking about, but it was pleasant to be addressed in this adult manner. Maybe there were some good things about being a sixth-grader.

"Take these forms, for example," Mr. Lamonte said. "In order to control for variables, put them in the front pouch of your backpacks immediately. The moment you get home, give them to your parent or legal guardian for signature. The moment the forms are signed, replace them in the front pouch of your backpacks."

He swept the room with another Lamonte Look.

"Then you won't have to think about them anymore," he said. "You will have controlled for all possible variables, and all the forms will be returned tomorrow. Does this make sense?"

Heads around the room nodded in unison. The concept of controlling for variables was obviously a powerful one. Julia Gillian watched as hands gathered up forms and placed them in the front pouches of backpacks. It was as if Mr. Lamonte had hypnotized them.

"You are now middle schoolers," Mr. Lamonte repeated. "Controlling for variables will help you manage your many new responsibilities. Let's all try to rise to the occasion, shall we?"

Shall we?

Shall we?

The "shall we?" whispers rose about the classroom like the rustling of small invisible animals. Julia Gillian bit down on her tongue in an effort to stay silent.

Julia Gillian was more than ready for lunch when the bell finally rang. Mr. Lamonte had not been kidding when he said their lives, now that they were sixth-graders, were fundamentally altered. After homeroom with Mr. Lamonte, they had moved to Math and from there to Social Studies and from there to Language Arts. And the day was only half over.

"How do they expect us to keep this all straight?" said Cerise, plunking her tray of Teriyaki Tots down on the table.

"I've already messed up," said Lathrop sadly. "I went to Social Studies when I was supposed to be in Art. And then I went to Language Arts when I was supposed to be in Social Studies."

This was not surprising for Lathrop, who was not an organized person, but still . . .

Julia Gillian, Bonwit, Cerise, and Lathrop always ate lunch together at the same table. It was a relief to be there now. Julia Gillian opened her lunch bag and peeked at the tiny folded lunch note inside.

The note was from her father, of course, since

Julia Gillian is my favorite middle-schooler of all time. From a Secret Admirer

he was the one who had made her lunch today. Still, it was always nice to have a lunch note to look forward to.

"What's the face of the day?" Cerise said, peering at Bonwit's lunch bag.

As usual, Bonwit's mother had drawn a face on his lunch bag with Magic Marker. The face was happy, but one eyebrow was raised quizzically, as if Bonwit's mother was asking how the day was going. She was an artist. She didn't have much time for painting these days, because Bonwit's baby twin sisters, Francine and Georgia, who were also known as the Tiny Tornadoes, were only ten months old, but she still found time to draw faces on his lunch bags.

"Addled," said Bonwit.

This was such a good word that Julia Gillian had to laugh. She and Bonwit looked at each other and, at the

same exact moment, made faces. This was something

they often did, and it was always fun, because Bonwit

could stretch his mouth extremely wide, and Julia Gillian

could roll her eyes almost all the way back into her head.

They had been making these faces since kindergarten.

Mrs. K, the beloved Lake Harriet lunch lady, came tapping her way down to their table with her dog-head cane.

"Well hello, Julia Gillian," she said.

"Hello, Mrs. K."

"How's my true dog person?"

"Fine."

"And how's Bigfoot?"

"Terrific," said Julia Gillian.

Mrs. K nodded and smiled. Then she winked at Julia Gillian, and Julia Gillian winked back. She had been practicing her winking for years, and she was finally getting truly good at it. Soon it would be time to add "Skilled at the Art of Winking" to the list of accomplishments she kept in a notebook under her mattress.

"How old is Bigfoot now?" said Cerise, when Mrs. K had tapped her way to the next table.

"Same as me. Eleven."

"That's old for a dog, isn't it?"

Julia Gillian supposed it was, but Bigfoot was strong and healthy, even if he was getting a little slow. She privately considered it unfair that children were not allowed to bring their dogs to school. If only dogs could spend the school days with their children, everyone would have more fun. Just thinking about Bigfoot sent a wave of missing him through her. She looked forward to going home, where Bigfoot would be waiting for her just inside the apartment door, his tongue hanging out and his tail wagging.

CHAPTER TWO
Their Laughter
Rang Out Loudly

The final lunch bell rang, which meant that it was time for recess. Now that they were sixth-graders, they didn't have to walk single file, nor did they have to use the buddy system. Right down the hall and out the playground door they went.

"I feel so free," Bonwit whispered.

Ever since last December, when the Tiny Tornadoes had been born, Bonwit had taken to whispering. Francine and Georgia were fussy babies, always in need of a nap and quick to wake up screaming. Consequently the Keller family had grown used to tiptoeing and whispering, and sometimes the habit spilled over into the world outside their house.

"We don't have to whisper," Julia Gillian reminded Bonwit, in a slightly louder than normal voice.

Cerise and Lathrop caught up to them on the edge of the playground, where they stood looking at the swings and rings and climbing tower that, just last year, they would have already been playing on. Secretly Julia Gillian really wanted to swing, but now that she was a sixth-grader, she wasn't sure if she should. Would that be babyish? Bonwit and Cerise and Lathrop seemed to be hesitating, too. All four of them pushed at the wood chips with the toes of their sneakers. They were sixth-graders now, after all, and their lives were

fundamentally altered. They weren't exactly sure what they should do.

"Look at those Crazy Eights," said Cerise. Her voice sounded uncertain, which was unusual for her. She pointed at the far end of the blacktop, where a group of eighth-grade boys and girls were playing dodgeball.

"They're loud," said Bonwit. "They're louder than the Tiny Tornadoes, even."

The Crazy Eights *were* loud. And chattery. Their laughter rang out. They dominated the entire playground. Julia Gillian felt a little afraid of them. The dodgeballs were being thrown quite hard, but none of the eighth-graders seemed to mind. They were all laughing as they dashed about. Julia Gillian wondered if, by the time you made it to eighth grade, you were tough. These eighth-graders certainly seemed to be.

Throw. Bounce. Hit.

Shrieks of laughter echoed over the playground.

"I'm scared of them," said Bonwit.

"So am I," said Cerise.

"Me, too," said Julia Gillian.

"I'm not," said Lathrop, but they all knew he was lying.

Phew. It was always good to know that you weren't the only one. And truly, the eighth-graders were fearsome, with their tallness, their loudness, their oldness, and the fact that next year, they would be in high school, which was an unimaginably huge and overwhelming place.

"What was Mr. Lamonte talking about with that variables stuff?" said Lathrop.

"All you need to know about that is this: Bring your forms back tomorrow," said Cerise.

Lathrop, who did not have a good track record with regard to forms, looked glum. "How many free throws are you up to now, Julia Gillian?" he asked, changing the subject.

"She's up to 103," said Bonwit, who had spent much of the summer watching Julia Gillian practice her free throws.

At the end of last year, Julia Gillian had decided that she wanted to be listed in the *Guinness Book of World Records* as a free-throw world champion. A doctor in California currently held the record — 2,740, which was a nearly inconceivable number — but why shouldn't there be a second category, for the Youngest Person Ever to Make the Most Free Throws in a Row? This category didn't actually exist, but Julia Gillian saw no reason why it shouldn't.

"One hundred and three?" said Lathrop. "Wow."

Julia Gillian shrugged. One hundred and three in a row was good, but it was nowhere near her ultimate goal of 363. Now a thought occurred to her. Perhaps she could use the principle of controlling for variables to help with her free throws. If she cut out all outside influences and focused only on her goal of making one shot after another, maybe she would reach her goal faster.

"If only we had a free-throw team," said Lathrop.

All four of them turned back to the dodgeball game. *Throw. Hit. Laugh.*

"If only we had a table tennis team," said Bonwit, who excelled at table tennis.

"If only we had a macaroni-eating team," said Cerise, whose favorite hot lunch was macaroni and cheese.

Just then, the end-of-recess whistle blew. Now that they were sixth-graders, recess was only twenty minutes long. They stared at one another.

"We didn't even play!" said Cerise.

"All we did was stand here," said Bonwit.

"And watch the scary Crazy Eights," said Julia Gillian.

Mr. Lamonte stood by the playground door, circling both arms in an exaggerated slow-motion wheel. They had wasted their entire recess. Life was indeed fundamentally altered. Back inside they went.

Last year, as fifth-graders whose classes were on the first floor, Bonwit and Julia Gillian had often glanced up the stairs that led to the second floor, which belonged to the sixth- and seventh-graders. Beyond that was the third floor, which was the sole province of the eighth-graders, where few other students dared to tread. They had run their hands up and down the polished wooden banister as far as they could reach. They had watched as the eighth-graders strode up their stairs, talking with their loud, confident voices.

The Sixlets and Sevvies were middle schoolers, too, of course, but the Crazy Eights ruled the school. It was common knowledge.

Now Julia Gillian and Bonwit and Cerise and Lathrop headed upstairs to the second floor. Julia Gillian glanced down at the first floor, where Ms. Schultz's room was. She and Bonwit had been in Ms. Schultz's class together last year. She thought of her desk near the back of the class. She pictured the *Vince Knows All* inscription that had been dug into it. Fifth grade had not been the easiest of years for Julia Gillian, but suddenly she missed it with all her heart.

"Come on, Julia Gillian," said Bonwit. "We can't be late."

"Yes, let's hurry, *shall we?*" said Cerise.

They made their way up the stairs, keeping to the far right. The right was the going-up side, and the left was the coming-down side. That was the rule with stairs at

Lake Harriet School, and it was a good rule, because otherwise, the stairs would be mayhem. All the Lake Harriet students were familiar with the going-up/coming-down rule, because Principal Smartt lectured them on it annually.

"Imagine a small third-grader trying to make it from the first floor to the second in order to deliver a note from his teacher," she said each year at the beginning of her Welcome to Lake Harriet assembly. "Carefully making his way up the right-hand side of the stairs, just as he has been taught. And now imagine a teeming mass of eighth-graders, pounding down *the wrong side of the stairs.*"

At this point, Principal Smartt would look slowly

about the gym, which was filled with Lake Harriet students.

"*SMUSH*," she would say, in a calm but extremely frightening voice.

For some reason, Julia Gillian had always pictured Bonwit as the smushed third-grader. It was a terrible image, and no matter how Julia Gillian had tried to erase it over the years, it had stayed with her.

Principal Smartt's lecture must have made an impression on Bonwit and Cerise, and even Lathrop, because they, too, were carefully keeping to the going up side of the stairs.

But not everyone was.

"Sixlets!"

"Sixlets!"

"Sixlets!"

A teeming mass of eighth-graders came pounding down the stairs with no regard for the rule. Julia Gillian and Bonwit and Cerise immediately flattened themselves against the right-hand wall.

"Out of the way, Sixlets!"

This came from a merry girl with a cloud of frizzy blond hair that floated behind her. She wore a monkey-head necklace and a T-shirt with a picture of a roaring hamster. She was tall. She was laughing. She was an eighth-grader. It was hard to imagine that this girl had ever been afraid of anything. Unlike Julia Gillian.

Was it going to be like this all year?

CHAPTER THREE

Controlling for Variables

"I think it'll be fine once we get adjusted," said Bonwit. "Don't you?"

It had been a day awash in newness, and Julia Gillian was glad to be in the fresh air with her best friend, making their way home on their long, familiar walk. They were at the Intersection of Fear, at the corner of Richfield Road and Lake Calhoun Parkway, waiting patiently for the image of the little white walking person to appear in the crosswalk box so that they could cross.

"I guess so," said Julia Gillian.

There was the little white walking person. They crossed the double lanes of the parkway. It was a sunny, windy day, and windsurfers were scudding back and forth across the white-capped lake.

"Still, though," said Bonwit.

"Still," agreed Julia Gillian.

She could tell that Bonwit was thinking about the eighth-graders. As best friends, they could often read each other's minds. Julia Gillian recalled the first time she had ever seen Bonwit. He had been dragged into the kindergarten classroom by his mother, Mrs. Keller. He was crying, and his knee was bleeding. The entire kindergarten class had watched in fascination as Bonwit's mother pried his fingers, one by one, off her hand.

"He scraped his knee on the steps," Mrs. Keller had said. "Trust me, he'll stop crying the minute I'm out the door."

The kindergartners' fascination had turned to horror — Bonwit's mother was leaving him? While his knee was still bleeding? While he was still crying? — but she had turned out to be correct. The minute she left the room, Bonwit had stopped crying and begun sucking his index and middle fingers instead. The teacher had given him a Band-Aid and then showed him the chair next to Julia Gillian, and Julia Gillian had shown him a photo of her dog, Bigfoot, which she had carried to school in her new kindergarten backpack.

Thus the friendship had begun, lo those many years ago.

"The eighth-graders are scary," said Julia Gillian now, which was the simple truth. The real question was what, if anything, they could do about it.

"Do you think we can just avoid them all year?" said Bonwit.

"No."

It was a nice idea, but there was simply no way to avoid the eighth-graders. They shared the same recess. They used the same stairs, and the same bathrooms. They were in middle school together.

"What are we going to do, then?" said Bonwit.

Julia Gillian shifted her backpack, which was much heavier now that she was a sixth-grader with big middle school textbooks, and an idea came to her. She thought of Principal Smartt's yearly lecture: If you always kept to your right while going up or coming down the stairs, the chance that a small third-grader would be smushed was greatly reduced. That was a way of controlling for variables, was it not? She was glad that Mr. Lamonte had brought up the concept.

"We're going to control for variables," she said.

"How?"

"Lots of ways. For example, if we never go to the bathroom at school, we'll never have to go up to the eighth-grade floor."

Earlier that day, she and Bonwit and Cerise and Lathrop had privately admitted to one another their fear of going to the bathroom. If they were still in fifth grade, they wouldn't have thought twice, because each elementary school classroom had its own bathroom. But sixth grade was an entirely different matter. The only middle school bathrooms were on the dreaded third floor.

"Never go to the bathroom at school?" said Bonwit. "Ever?"

Admittedly this would be a hard variable to control

for. While it was true that neither of them had had to use the bathroom today, that was very unusual.

"It's worth a try," said Julia Gillian.

They had reached the intersection of 36th and Dupont. Julia Gillian turned left, toward the apartment where she lived with her parents and Bigfoot, and Bonwit kept walking straight, toward the house where he lived with his artist mother, his carpenter father, and Francine and Georgia, the Tiny Tornadoes.

"You think of other middle school variables tonight," said Julia Gillian. "And I'll do the same. We'll make a list tomorrow."

Now that she understood the concept, Julia Gillian wondered if she could become accomplished at the Art of Controlling for Variables. Then she would be able to add "Skilled at the Art of Controlling for Variables" to the ever-growing list of accomplishments that she kept underneath her mattress. She decided to start working on her variable-controlling immediately, beginning with her daily free-throw practice. If she was going to make it into the *Guinness Book of World Records*, then she needed all the help she could get.

At the door to her apartment, she fished out the key that she kept on a shoelace around her neck.

"Well hello, Bigfoot."

Bigfoot was waiting for her, his skinny brown stuffed bat in his mouth, his long, brushy tail sweeping slowly back and forth. Bigfoot had been her steadfast companion all her life, and Julia Gillian had long

wondered whether he had a sixth sense for exactly when she would be returning home. Now he looked up at her and coughed. It was a soft little cough, and Julia Gillian wondered if he had a cold. Did dogs get colds? She wasn't sure.

She thought about Cerise's comment. Bigfoot was eleven years old now, which was indeed quite old for a dog, especially a St. Bernard. He moved more slowly than he used to, and it was harder for him to climb up onto Julia Gillian's bed. He spent much of his time lying on his long magenta pillow, with his skinny brown stuffed bat under his chin.

"Would you like to shoot some free throws with me, Dog of My Dreams?"

As a dog, Bigfoot was of course incapable of shooting free throws, but Julia Gillian didn't want him to feel left out. And the truth was that he did seem to enjoy lying in the shade of the lilac bushes behind the apartment building and observing while she practiced her free throws. Julia Gillian's parents would be home soon from their schools, but while they were away it was nice to have Bigfoot with her, even if she was just in the back alley. With her dog by her side, she was never lonely.

Julia Gillian and Bigfoot made their way down the back stairs and out the back door of their building. A basketball hoop hung off the garage next to the alley. Julia Gillian hugged her basketball to her chest and looked up at the living room window of the apartment just below her own, where her friend Enzo lived with her brother, Zap. Enzo was a student at Metropolitan State University, and she was often at home, reading large books. Zap was in his last year of studying to be a chef at the Dunwoody Culinary

Institute, and he, too, was often at home, trying out recipes of his own creation.

Sometimes Julia Gillian could see Enzo or Zap pass by the window, and in nice weather, like today, their living room window was often open to the breeze, so that the curtains fluttered. Enzo and Zap and Julia Gillian had been friends for most of Julia Gillian's life, and when she had a problem, she knew she could count on Enzo to help her. This was one of the many things that Julia Gillian liked about living in an apartment building. Her friends were always close by.

"Are we ready, Bigfoot?"

Bigfoot thumped his tail twice from the shade of the

lilac bush, where he was lying in a shallow dirt trough. He had scratched out this dirt trough himself, back in the spring, and Julia Gillian admired the way it fit his long body perfectly.

"Today we'll be controlling for variables," she said, "so as to avoid an adverse outcome."

Julia Gillian still wasn't entirely sure what "adverse outcome" meant, but she liked the sound of it.

"We're going to stick to a routine and keep every-thing the same."

Bigfoot thumped his tail and settled his skinny stuffed bat under his jaw. Julia Gillian concentrated on her routine. First, she stood far behind the free-throw line and held the basketball with both hands spread wide to cover as much of the leatherette as possible. Next, she twirled the ball three times between her hands. Then, she bounced it three times up and down.

Julia Gillian advanced to the free-throw line and breathed deeply.

Each time she breathed in, she thought, *Basket*.

Each time she breathed out, she thought, *Ball*.

This was a simple chant, but Julia Gillian found it to

be highly effective. When she first began practicing free throws, she had made hardly any, but now she was up to 103 in a row. If she controlled for variables, who knew how high she might be able to go?

She eyed the rim of the hoop. She preferred to aim for the upper left-hand corner of the backboard, so that the ball could bounce off it and then glide through the hoop. Many people preferred the swish, in which the ball did not touch the backboard at all, but not Julia Gillian. She liked to hear the *thunk* of the ball hitting the backboard, followed by the airy rustle as it dropped through the net.

"Okay, Bigfoot, here we go."

He thumped his tail again. What an agreeable dog he was.

"Uno, dos, tres," said Julia Gillian.

Zap had taught her how to count in Spanish, and she liked to practice when she could. Zap also knew how to say *thank you* and *you're welcome* in ten different languages. Julia Gillian crouched down and then, with both legs, sprang up and flung the ball straight toward the backboard.

Thunk, swish.

"And we're off!" said Julia Gillian to Bigfoot, who opened his eyes and thumped his tail.

CHAPTER FOUR

Did We Interrupt You?

Thunk, swish.

Thunk, swish.

Thunk, swish.

Julia Gillian barely had to move. She had her free-throw routine down to a science. So accustomed was Julia Gillian to the slight slant of the alley, the angle of the garage overhang, the position of the backboard, and the feel of the basketball in her hands, that she was like a human free-throw-shooting machine. The routine was hypnotic. So this was what controlling for variables felt like.

Ball, crouch, fling, *thunk, swish.* Ball, crouch, fling, *thunk, swish.*

Now she was up to 11.

Now she was up to 27.

Now she was up to 43, and she felt as if she could go forever, as if today might be the day that she again reached 103. Not only would she reach 103, but she would surpass 103. Nothing would stand in her way. She could feel it in her bones.

"Hi, honey."

"Hi, sweetie."

Thunk, BONK.

Julia Gillian turned to see her mother and father standing beside Bigfoot, who in his sleep had extended his front paws to their full length in front of him.

"Oh, dear," said Julia Gillian's mother. "Did we interrupt you?"

Julia Gillian picked up her basketball, which had rolled across the alley and nosed up against Mr. Hoffbeck's garbage can. She took a deep breath. Yes, her parents had interrupted her. She didn't want to be annoyed with them, but didn't it seem logical that if you came across someone in an alley who was obviously concentrating hard on controlling for variables, you shouldn't speak to her? You shouldn't even think of walking past her. What you should do is put everything on hold, stand perfectly still, and remain silent.

"A little," said Julia Gillian.

"Sorry," said her father. "We just got home from school and we thought that a game of MEERKAT would be fun."

"Okay."

Julia Gillian didn't want to play MEERKAT, which was the Gillian family's variation on HORSE, but she also didn't want to hurt her parents' feelings.

"Great!" said her father. "I'll begin."

Julia Gillian looked at Bigfoot, lying in his dirt trough with his eyes half-closed, and she beamed a prediction to him telepathically: *Dad will now do his special layup.* Bigfoot thumped his tail twice in rapid succession, which was his usual response to a Julia Gillian telepathic thought. He coughed his new little cough.

Thump, thump, thump, twist, leap, fling, *swish.*

"My special layup triumphs again!" said her father.

Now comes the special layup dance of triumph, beamed Julia Gillian to Bigfoot, who double-thumped his tail in response.

Sure enough, her father placed his index finger on the top of his head and twirled three times on the asphalt. Truly Julia Gillian was extremely Skilled at the Art of Knowing. When her father was finished twirling, he smiled at her. Julia Gillian smiled back but said nothing. She was rather tired of her father's special layup dance of triumph, but he loved doing it, and, of course, she didn't want to hurt his feelings.

"Your turn," said her father, and he bounced the ball to Julia Gillian.

She made a halfhearted attempt to replicate the special layup, which included a small leap in the middle of the dribble, but she was not successful.

"That's an *M*," said her father happily.

Although he would deny it if accused, he was a man who liked to win at MEERKAT whenever possible.

"Your turn," said Julia Gillian, and she bounced the ball to her mother.

She didn't try to beam a telepathic prediction to Bigfoot because her mother was not predictable. She was a wild card, as Enzo would say, a wild card who liked to mix it up and keep things lively. What sort of shot would she attempt today?

Julia Gillian's mother stood exactly where she had been standing when she caught the ball, which was far off to the left side of the basket. She planted her feet firmly, and without moving an inch and using her arms only, arced the basketball toward the basket. It didn't go in, but Julia Gillian appreciated her mother's willingness to try a difficult shot. It was usually her mother who got to the *T* of MEERKAT first. Julia Gillian respected the way she lost with such enthusiasm and good cheer.

Her father grabbed the ball and did another special shot, the one that he referred to as an over-under hangman noose. Julia Gillian looked over at Bigfoot, who was gazing at her with his head tilted to one side. She was sure that he sensed her impatience with this game of MEERKAT — couldn't her parents see that she was determined to work on her free throws? — and, as if to prove her right, he gave a little cough.

Luckily, today's game of MEERKAT ended quickly, due to Julia Gillian's mother and her many interesting but unsuccessful shots.

"See you inside, Julia Gillian," said her father, who was happy because he had won.

"See you inside," said her mother, who was never

unhappy at losing. "We'll call from the window when dinner's ready."

Finally Julia Gillian could go back to her free-throw practice. But now that her concentration had been broken, she couldn't seem to get past 41. That was one of the hazards of uncontrolled variables, such as your parents showing up in the middle of a good streak. Bigfoot watched from his shady dirt trough. He was a patient dog, willing to wait as long as it took.

CHAPTER FIVE

Are You My Reading Buddy?

"We'll take turns," said Julia Gillian. "You first."

The homeroom bell had not yet rung, and Bonwit and Julia Gillian were sitting at their desks in Mr. Lamonte's room, comparing their Controlling for Middle School Variables lists.

"Number one," said Bonwit. "Third-floor bathroom."

Actually it had been Julia Gillian who had come up with the bathroom variable. Yesterday, in fact, but she didn't want to argue, so she nodded and put a small check next to *bathroom* on her own list.

"And how do you suggest we control for it?" she said.

"Go before and after school, never during."

They looked at each other. This would be tough.

"There *is* that little bathroom outside the gym, by the lunchroom," said Julia Gillian. "If we get desperate."

The little one-stall bathroom was for use only during lunch or gym, but still, it was good to know that it was there.

"Number two," said Julia Gillian. "Free throws. Control for all free-throw variables possible."

Bonwit nodded. He was not trying to make it into the *Guinness Book of World Records*, so this rule didn't affect him, but he was a supportive friend.

"Number three," he said. "Stick to the right-hand side when going up or coming down the stairs."

This was one of Principal Smartt's basic rules, but it was an excellent one. Given that they had been forced to flatten themselves against the wall yesterday, Julia Gillian agreed that this variable should definitely be on the list.

"This'll do for starters," said Julia Gillian. "We'll add to it if we need to."

The bell rang, and Mr. Lamonte rapped his knuckles on the desk to get their attention.

"How many of you are familiar with the time-honored Lake Harriet tradition of the reading buddy?"

All the students raised their hands. Of course everyone knew about the reading buddy tradition. After all, they had all once been third-graders, hadn't they? And hadn't they each been matched with a sixth-grader who met with them once a week for the purpose of fostering a love of reading? And hadn't they all worked

on a reading buddy project for the Reading Buddy Extravaganza?

Julia Gillian remembered well her own reading buddy, Hilda Livingston, who had been a sixth-grade girl with unmoving hair and bangs cut so perfectly straight across her forehead that they looked painted on. This reading buddy had seemed to care only about horses, to the extent that every single book she wanted to read with Julia Gillian was about a horse. Julia Gillian didn't care much about horses. There was nothing wrong with them, but she herself was a dog person. It had been a long fall semester with Hilda Livingston.

"Excellent," said Mr. Lamonte. "The reading buddy tradition is one of my personal favorites, and I am happy to announce that today you will each meet with your reading buddy for the first time."

Julia Gillian looked at Bonwit, who made a sad face back at her. He knew that she disliked reading and had not been looking forward to being a reading buddy. Bonwit, on the other hand, loved to read and had been stockpiling some of his former favorite books in hopes that his third-grader would love them as much as he had. Bonwit was trying to train the Tiny Tornadoes into being readers, too. This was admittedly tough going, as Francine and Georgia were far more interested in shrieking, eating, and batting at their matching farm animal mobiles than in listening to books, but Bonwit was determined.

"As sixth-graders, it is your responsibility to foster a love of reading in your third-grade buddy," said Mr. Lamonte. "Reading is fundamental, and the teachers of Lake Harriet are counting on you to be a good influence on your third-grader."

There it was again: *Reading is fundamental.* Julia Gillian's parents, both of whom loved to read, had been telling her this all her life. And now Mr. Lamonte had added the *As sixth-graders* phrase he was so fond of using. But what if you didn't like to read? What if you weren't capable of being a good influence on a third-grader?

Julia Gillian liked to make things. She liked to dream up new projects and then carry them out. She didn't mind getting her hands dirty, and she liked to refine her methods until she had perfected them. Reading didn't have enough action for her.

"Why does it always have to be reading?" Julia Gillian whispered to Bonwit. "Why can't it ever be papier-mâché mask making instead?"

Julia Gillian excelled at the Art of Papier-Mâché Mask Making. In fact, it was one of her best talents. "Skilled at the Art of Papier-Mâché Mask Making" had long ago been added to the sheet of notebook paper on which she listed her accomplishments. She was quite sure that "Skilled at the Art of Being a Reading Buddy" was never going to make it onto the list.

"You know how they are about reading," said Bonwit.

His tone was matter-of-fact. He was right. Every adult seemed to believe the same thing, which was that reading was fundamental, and every child should love to read. As a book lover himself, and as a brother trying to train his baby sisters into book-loving, Bonwit was firmly on their side.

But the fact of the matter was that not every child *did* love to read, thought Julia Gillian. She herself was proof of this. She had once, the summer before fourth grade, come across a book that she had high hopes for — a green book with a picture of a dog on the front cover — but it had ended up being a very sad book, and Julia Gillian didn't like to think about it.

"Without further ado, it is time to meet your third-grader," said Mr. Lamonte. "And here they are."

He opened the door and a line of third-graders filed into the classroom. They lined up in front of the board with their teacher, Ms. Pennyfeather, shooing them down to make room. Julia Gillian had the urge to laugh. Had she ever been that small? Had she ever looked so nervous? No wonder Principal Smartt emphasized the smushability of the third-graders in her yearly stairs lecture. These poor little things. One of them was chewing his thumbnail as if it were a piece of licorice, and another was yanking at a long strand of hair. Yank. Yank. Yank.

"I hope I don't get that hair yanker," Julia Gillian whispered to Bonwit. "That would drive me crazy."

"I don't want the nail biter," said Bonwit.

Despite the fact that when he was nervous he picked at his own thumbnails, Bonwit hated nail biting. He was in general a calm and kind person, even around his screaming baby sisters, but nail biters immediately set him on edge. Mr. Lamonte and Ms. Pennyfeather huddled together, comparing notes on the sheets of paper they each held. The third-graders shuffled and fidgeted.

They looked a bit like suspects in a large police lineup.

"Third-graders, when your name is called, please go to the desk of your reading buddy," said Mr. Lamonte. "Today will be a get-to-know-you day."

Good, thought Julia Gillian. She had been afraid that she would have to jump right into being a good reading influence, and she wasn't sure how she was going to do that.

"Bonwit Keller, your reading buddy is Judith Montpelier," said Mr. Lamonte.

The hair yanker took a step forward from the line. Yank. Her nerve failed her, and she stepped back.

"Go on, Judith," urged Ms. Pennyfeather.

"Raise your hand, Bonwit, so that your reading buddy knows where you are," said Mr. Lamonte.

Bonwit raised his hand. He shot a quick look at Julia Gillian. He had gotten the hair yanker, but at least he was spared the nail biter.

"Cerise Cronin, your reading buddy is Mimi Frank," said Mr. Lamonte.

A girl, extraordinarily tall for third grade, stepped smartly forward. Her socks were mismatched, but they were so wildly mismatched that Julia Gillian suspected the mismatching was on purpose. This girl seemed as bold as Cerise. Cerise pumped both fists in the air, and the tall third-grader smiled and nodded. A perfect match.

And so it went. Lathrop was matched with a small, sharp-eyed, unsmiling girl who seemed as if she would keep him toeing the line. The row of third-graders grew shorter, and Julia Gillian grew more nervous. What if she was paired with a true reader, someone who would expect her to have vast amounts of knowledge of great books?

"Julia Gillian, your reading buddy is Fergus Cannon," said Mr. Lamonte.

A boy stepped forward. He was so short and slight that Julia Gillian hadn't even noticed him in the lineup despite the fact that his sneakers were bright red. His hair was black and stuck straight up from his head. How had this Fergus Cannon gotten his hair to stick straight up? And why did he have such a suspicious look on his face? Despite his small size, there was something intimidating about Fergus Cannon. Julia Gillian was not at all sure that she wanted to get to know him. But there was nothing she could do about it. Bonwit, to her right, was already engaged in lively conversation with Judith Montpelier. Grudgingly Julia Gillian raised her hand, and Fergus Cannon walked toward her.

"And there we go," said Mr. Lamonte. "Let's get to know each other, shall we?"

Fergus Cannon stopped in front of Julia Gillian's desk. He said nothing, and neither did she. He looked at her, and she looked at him, and then she looked down at his bright red sneakers. Silence mounted between them. All around them, sixth-graders and third-graders were chattering away, while their wall of silence grew higher. Julia Gillian looked back up at Fergus, who was gazing directly at her. His eyes were wide open. Did this boy ever blink?

"Hello," said Julia Gillian.

One of them had to say something, and it might as well be her. She was stuck with this third-grader. Like it or not, he was hers for the entire fall. They would have to read together, and they would have to complete a Reading Buddy Extravaganza project together.

"I hate to read," said Fergus Cannon.

His voice was flat and determined. He looked straight at Julia Gillian as if he expected her to argue with him. Bonwit and his reading buddy, Judith Montpelier, broke off their animated conversation and turned their heads toward Julia Gillian. Here was a third-grader who not only hated to read, but was open about it.

Silence fell among the nearby desks. Julia Gillian could sense her friends holding their breath. It was no secret that she herself didn't much care for books. What would she do, stuck as she was with this recalcitrant child as her reading buddy? How would she handle this situation? What could she possibly say?

"Welcome to the club," said Julia Gillian.

CHAPTER SIX
The Sixlet Is Down

The third-graders and Ms. Pennyfeather had returned to their own classroom, and Mr. Lamonte was passing out the set of weekly math challenge problems.

"Feel free to work in groups," he said. "Let's focus, shall we?"

The class was already used to the repeated "shall we?" Even Cerise only repeated it once, and under her breath.

"The third-graders will be back next week," said Mr. Lamonte. "Your first reading buddy assignment is to bring in a book that you think your buddy might enjoy. Try to match the book to your buddy's personality."

This was not going to be easy. What sort of book would possibly appeal to a buddy who hated to read?

Bonwit gave Julia Gillian a sympathetic glance. His own task would be easy, as his buddy, Judith Montpelier, had told him that she was a voracious reader who had been reading silently since she was four years old. Judith also preferred books without illustrations, which made no sense at all to Julia Gillian. There had been a time long ago — when all the books she owned were picture books — when Julia Gillian actually did love books. But adults expected you to grow out of that phase, and move on to silent reading of non-illustrated books. The problem was that Julia Gillian still liked picture books. What was so wrong with that?

She tried to focus on her math challenge sheet, but the unblinking eyes and gravity-defying hair of Fergus Cannon kept appearing in her mind.

"What are you going to do about your reading buddy?" whispered Bonwit.

"I have no idea. He hates to read."

"So do you," Cerise pointed out.

This was true, but it was of no help. If only Bonwit had been matched with Fergus Cannon. Julia Gillian felt strongly that she would have been able to bluff her way through the fall with Judith Montpelier, who was a talker. All Julia Gillian would need to do was sit back and let her talk on and on about all the non-illustrated books she had read silently in the previous week.

But now a greater problem presented itself.

"What's wrong?" said Bonwit. "You're twitching."

Julia Gillian gave him a look.

"Uh-oh," said Bonwit. "Variable Number One?"

They had been friends for so long that few words were necessary. Julia Gillian nodded.

"You can't hold it?"

"No."

At that, Cerise looked up. She, too, had joined in the Variable #1 vow. They were all afraid of what might happen to them, up on the third floor. Who knew what the eighth-graders might do to you? The moment you set foot on the first step of the stairs that separated the eighth-graders from the rest of humanity, all bets were off.

But there was no getting around it this time. The bathroom by the gym was closed for the day because of a plumbing problem — probably due to overuse — and Julia Gillian would have to brave the third floor. She rose from her seat and walked to Mr. Lamonte's desk and picked up the bathroom pass, which was a plastic dog bone with a long piece of yarn threaded through a hole drilled in one end. Before she left the classroom, she looked back at Bonwit.

Good luck, he mouthed.

She nodded.

Out the door. Down the hall. Now she stood before the stairs to the third floor. Above her were the eighth-graders, sitting in their sixth-hour classrooms. But surely a few of them would be out and about: carrying a note from one teacher to another, getting a drink, retrieving an item from one of their eighth-grade lockers, which were taller and wider than the sixth-grade lockers.

Or going to the bathroom.

For a moment, Julia Gillian considered retreating. She could run down to the first floor and try to slip into the teachers' bathroom. She would be quick. No one would even see her. Or would they? What if an actual teacher was in the teachers' bathroom? That idea was so horrifying that Julia Gillian felt a little dizzy.

A couple of years ago, at a time when Julia Gillian was scared, Enzo had once told her that sometimes the only way out was through. Julia Gillian knew what she had to do.

Step one.

She slid all the way over to the far right and clutched the banister with both hands. It was made of dark wood, highly polished. For a moment, she considered

the life of the banister. How many Lake Harriet students
had grasped its shining surface on their way up or down
the stairs? How often did the custodians polish it? Of
what sort of wood was it carved?

You're stalling, said Julia Gillian to herself. *The only way out is through.*

Step two. Three. Four. Five.

Now the top of the stairs was visible, and so were the legs of the piano that Mr. Mixler, the music teacher, played every morning as the students came pouring in. The piano used to be on the first-floor landing, but over the summer it had been moved to the third floor so that the sound drifted down the stairs, welcoming the Lake Harriet students as they walked into the school. Julia Gillian loved Mr. Mixler, who was also her trumpet teacher, and she loved his piano music in the early morning, but this was not the early morning, and Mr. Mixler was nowhere in sight.

Six. Seven. Eight. Nine.

And here she was, on the eighth-grade floor, in uncharted territory. The bathroom was halfway down the hall on the right, and Julia Gillian fixed her eyes upon it. She kept her gaze straight ahead.

Left, right, left.

Left, right, left.

Was this how it felt to be a soldier going into battle?

WOMEN.

Women? Was this what happened in eighth grade? Were you no longer a girl? Julia Gillian wasn't sure she would ever be ready for eighth grade. She breathed in — *basket* — and breathed out — *ball*, and reached out to push open the swinging door, when —

Smack!

— it swung out and hit her in the shoulder.

Ouch.

"Yikes!"

"Did we just hit that Sixlet with the door?"

"Sixlet? Are you okay?"

"Is the Sixlet alive?"

"The Sixlet's not speaking!"

"Do we need to call 911?"

The eighth-grade voices swirled above Julia Gillian, who was crouched on the floor, holding her hurting shoulder. Alive? Not speaking? Call 911?

This had to stop. *The only way out is through.* Julia Gillian rose to her feet.

"Excuse me," she said, and marched through the swirl of eighth-grade girls — there appeared to be several hundred of them, with that tall, frizzy-haired one front and center — and straight into the bathroom.

CHAPTER SEVEN

In One Fell Swoop

Julia Gillian sat in the stall for a while after she went to the bathroom. It was quiet. Outside the bathroom door she could hear the occasional sounds of footsteps and voices, but she stayed still so as to calm herself after the frightening encounter. She took a deep breath in — *basket* — and let a deep breath out — *ball.* Then she washed her hands, dried them under the blower, and redid her ponytail. *You're stalling,* she told herself again. *Courage.*

Julia Gillian took another deep breath, pushed open the swinging door of the bathroom, and emerged into the eighth grade hallway. She looked right: no one. She looked left.

Gulp.

"Hello."

It was the tall eighth-grader with the cloud of frizzy blond hair, the one who had been wearing the roaring hamster T-shirt and the monkey-head necklace the other day. The one who had laughed merrily as Julia Gillian, Bonwit, Lathrop, and Cerise flattened themselves against the wall on the stairs.

"Do you speak English?" said the girl, and she laughed.

Today she was wearing a gray T-shirt with a picture of a red balloon on it. This reminded Julia Gillian of *The Red Balloon*, which was a book about a French boy and his red balloon. It had been one of her very

favorite books back in the days of picture books. For a minute she wondered if she could bring it in for Fergus Cannon. No. As a third-grader, he would be expected to have moved on past the picture-book phase, too. How unfair.

"Do you understand the meaning of the word *hello*?" said the girl.

"Hello," said Julia Gillian warily.

It was obvious

that this eighth-grader had been lying in wait for her. Wasn't it enough that the gang of Crazy Eights had slammed into her on their way out of the bathroom? Julia Gillian fervently wished that she could telepathically transport herself back down the stairs and into Mr. Lamonte's room, where Bonwit had probably already finished the math challenge problems without her.

"I've seen you around, you know," said the girl. "You're the one who's always out walking your dog. The St. Bernard."

Now Julia Gillian looked up. She was indeed always out walking her dog, and her dog was a St. Bernard. This frightening girl knew something personal about her. Just then, someone came up the stairs from the second floor two steps at a time. It was Mr. Mixler. In fact,

she had Trumpet class in just a few minutes. Mr. Mixler
was carrying his ever-present baton, which was known
as the Mixler baton, and he
danced it through the air
in delight.

"Two of my favorite
students in one fell
swoop!" said Mr. Mixler.
"Ms. Caravaggio, just in
case you haven't yet had
the pleasure, please meet
Ms. Gillian, trumpet player
and all-around interesting
person. Ms. Gillian, please
meet Ms. Caravaggio, terrific

trumpet player, captain of the Lake Harriet Lady Dragons basketball team, excellent math student, and all-round accomplished person."

Julia Gillian frowned. She couldn't help herself. The way Mr. Mixler described Ms. Caravaggio, she sounded like a perfect person. Next to all Ms. Caravaggio's accomplishments, not to mention her supreme self-confidence and her eighth-graderness, Julia Gillian felt dull and unskilled. This was an unpleasant feeling.

"Well, got to go," said Julia Gillian. This sounded somewhat rude, even to her own ears, but Ms. Caravaggio smiled and inclined her head. *She's just trying to be gracious in front of Mr. Mixler,* thought Julia Gillian, and she hurried down the stairs.

Usually Julia Gillian loved trumpet lessons — Mr. Mixler was her favorite teacher, and she and Bonwit planned to become world-famous jazz trumpeters — but they were studying music theory this week, and music theory was not nearly as much fun as actually playing the trumpet. Ms. Caravaggio, of course, as a fourth-year trumpet student, probably not only excelled at music theory but loved it. Julia Gillian shook her head.

Bonwit was bent over his music theory worksheet, filling in quarter notes and eighth notes with a #2 pencil, when Julia Gillian finally made it to Mr. Mixler's classroom. He looked up, dramatically wiped his brow to show his relief at the sight of her, and removed his red

Sharpie from his pencil case. Bonwit and Julia Gillian were both fans of Sharpies. When they were younger, they had spent years in the wasteland of washable markers, and now that Sharpies were finally allowed, they both used them whenever possible. Bonwit wrote her a note.

you were gone a long time

Julia Gillian nodded. She had indeed been gone a long time. She got out her own favorite Sharpie, which was brown and almost new, and wrote back.

THEY GANGED UP ON ME!!!...

"Are you okay?" Bonwit whispered. "Did they hurt you?"

"They called me a Sixlet. They knocked me to the ground. And they hurt my shoulder."

This was an exaggeration, of course, but the minute she heard herself saying the words, Julia Gillian believed them. What a terrible experience she had just been through. Cerise, who had overheard her, was making a face of sympathy and horror. Now that Julia Gillian was safely in Mr. Mixler's classroom, she could relax.

"What did they do then?" whispered Bonwit.

"They laughed," said Julia Gillian.

She pictured herself, a poor sixth-grader, cowering on the floor while the eighth-grade girls capered about as if she were their human sacrifice. She reached up and

rubbed her left shoulder while Bonwit looked at her with
eyes full of concern. Wait, was her left shoulder the one
that had been injured? No, it had been her right shoulder.
Well, too late now. Julia Gillian continued to rub the
wrong, uninjured shoulder.

"Also," said Julia Gillian, "one of them knows who I am. She knows who Bigfoot is. She's seen us around."

"That's not good," said Bonwit.

"Her name is Ms. Caravaggio," said Julia Gillian. "She's mean. She's probably a dog hater."

There was nothing worse than a dog hater, in Julia Gillian's opinion. How could anyone hate a dog? Especially a beautiful old St. Bernard like Bigfoot. Ms. Caravaggio was probably spying on Julia Gillian every time she was out with Bigfoot. She might be sending rays of dog hatred toward them. At this thought, Julia Gillian was filled with sorrow for her dog, who had done nothing to deserve such treatment.

Mr. Mixler waved the Mixler baton in the air.

"How are you doing with your music theory worksheets?" he said. "Almost finished?"

Julia Gillian looked down at her worksheet. She hadn't filled in a single note. Meanwhile Bonwit was nearly finished. Resentment toward Ms. Caravaggio filled her. Not only had she been part of the eighth-grade gang outside the bathroom, but she was one of Mr. Mixler's favorite students. Julia Gillian wanted to be more favorite than Ms. Caravaggio, but compared with such a perfect person, how could she compete?

Oh, dear. She rubbed her uninjured shoulder again and sighed.

CHAPTER EIGHT

Entering the
Free-Throw Zone

It had been a difficult day. Variable #1 had not been controlled for, and the outcome had been adverse. Julia Gillian needed cheering up. When she got home, she decided to control for Variable #2 by practicing her free throws. Who knew, it was possible that today might be the day that she broke her personal world record of 103.

"Come, Bigfoot," she said to her dog, who, as usual, was waiting patiently for her just inside the apartment door. He wagged his tail twice and stood quietly while she clipped the leash to his collar, even though there was no need for it. Bigfoot would never run away.

"Are you ready for a walk, Dog of My Dreams?"

He looked up at her and coughed softly, then sneezed. Maybe he did have a cold. It was a good thing that his annual appointment with the Uptown Vet was scheduled for later that week.

"Bless you, Bigfoot. Let's see if Enzo is home before we practice our free throws, shall we?"

Shall we? Mr. Lamonte was rubbing off on Julia Gillian. They made their way down to the second floor, where Enzo and Zap lived. As usual, their shoes were lined up neatly outside their apartment door. Zap's were huge, and Enzo's, even her three pairs of platforms, were small. Julia Gillian knocked her special Enzo and Zap knock.

KNOCK. KNOCK. KNOCK.

KnockKnockKnock.

Knock. Knock. Knock.

"Noodlie!"

That was Enzo's special nickname for Julia Gillian, and every time she heard it, Julia Gillian felt happy. Enzo flung open the door and shook Julia Gillian's hand. They had known each other for most of Julia Gillian's life, but once in a while Enzo liked to shake hands as if they were meeting for the first time. Now she reached down and held out her hand to Bigfoot, who obligingly raised his right paw.

"We're on our way to the alley to control for variables," said Julia Gillian, who had explained the concept to Enzo.

"What are you up to now?"

"One hundred three."

"What's your ultimate goal, Noodlie?"

"Three hundred twelve."

"That's a lot of free throws in a row."

"It is," agreed Julia Gillian. "That doctor in California made 2,740, but I'm only eleven."

Youngest World Champion Free Thrower was a major goal, but Julia Gillian liked to aim high. She looked forward to adding "Skilled at the Art of the World Record Free Throw" to her list of accomplishments.

"Come, Bigfoot," she said, and she waved good-bye to Enzo.

Basket —

— ball.

Bounce. Bounce. Bounce. Crouch and fling.

One.

Two.

Three.

It usually took at least twelve free throws for Julia Gillian to feel herself entering the free-throw zone, and during that interim time she always hoped no one would come walking down the alley or driving past in a car. She didn't want any distractions. That was part of controlling for variables. She glanced up at Enzo's window for good luck, and there was Enzo, sitting out on her balcony with one of her thick Metropolitan State University textbooks propped in her lap. Enzo gave her a thumbs-up, and Julia Gillian nodded.

Four.

Five.

Six.

"Hello, Ms. Gillian."

BANG. The basketball hit the backboard and bounced off down the alley. Now Julia Gillian would have to move from her stationary position and chase it. Her concentration was broken, and she would have to start from scratch. She looked over at the intruder.

Oh no. Ms. Caravaggio. On a blue and silver bike,

one foot touching up and
down on the pavement
to keep herself balanced,
her nimbus of blond
hair rising in
the air
behind
her
helmet.

Ms. Caravaggio knew where Julia Gillian lived?
Maybe she was an eighth-grade stalker. *Don't move*, Julia

Gillian telepathically beamed to Bigfoot. There was no telling what a dog hater would do if she caught sight of him, snoozing in the shade with his stuffed bat under one paw.

Too late.

"There's your dog. What's his name?"

"Tiny."

Tiny? Where did that come from? It had just popped right out of Julia Gillian's mouth, and it was a lie. This was not good. Julia Gillian had gotten into trouble last year by lying. Since then, she had vowed not to lie anymore, and here she was, blatantly lying to this eighth-grader. Now Ms. Caravaggio doubled over, laughing.

"Tiny? Tiny!"

Bigfoot didn't even look up from his nap. He didn't

sccm bothered by all the laughing, but Julia Gillian found it insulting. Even though she didn't know his real name, Ms. Caravaggio was still laughing at Bigfoot.

"Want to play some one-on-one?" said Ms. Caravaggio.

She pantomimed shooting a basket. Julia Gillian shook her head. Ms. Caravaggio looked puzzled.

"But I've seen you practicing your free throws," said Ms. Caravaggio. "Maybe you should go out for the Lady Dragons."

Ms. Caravaggio was something of a legend at Lake Harriet. She had been captain of the team last year as a seventh-grader, when the position usually went to an eighth-grader, and the team had won the citywide middle school championship. For a moment, Julia Gillian thought again about all of Ms. Caravaggio's accomplishments.

1. She was an excellent trumpet player.
2. She was an excellent basketball player.
3. She was in Accelerated Math.
4. She had many friends.
5. She was one of Mr. Mixler's favorite students.
6. She was fearless.

Julia Gillian doubted whether Ms. Caravaggio had ever been afraid to use the bathroom on the eighth-grade floor. Indeed, Ms. Caravaggio appeared to lead a charmed life. Julia Gillian suddenly felt intensely jealous of Ms.

Caravaggio, who had probably never had a sad day in her life. She didn't appear to have a single regret, either, about almost smushing them on the stairs the other day, or about bashing Julia Gillian's shoulder with the eighth-grade bathroom door.

There was something heartless about Ms. Caravaggio, she decided, and no way would Julia Gillian be caught playing one-on-one with a dog-hating charmed life–leading eighth-grade stalker, a member of the gang of Crazy Eights who had thrown her to the floor outside the bathroom. Julia Gillian shook her head.

"No, thank you," she said.

There. She had controlled for Variable #2, and she had done so calmly and with dignity.

CHAPTER NINE
The Battle of the Book

"Guess what?" said Julia Gillian.

"What?" said Bonwit.

"I've got a problem."

"What is it?"

"Ms. Caravaggio knows where I live."

They were at lunch, sitting at their usual table near the back with Cerise and Lathrop. Word had spread about Julia Gillian's encounter with the eighth-grade girls in the bathroom. Some of the sixth-graders had decided immediately that they, too, would control for Variable #1. This meant that during lunch, the one-stall bathroom next to the gym was seeing a great deal of use.

"No way," said Lathrop.

"Seriously?" said Cerise.

"How do you know?" said Bonwit.

"She stalked me yesterday in the alley while I was practicing my free throws. And, she's captain of the Lady Dragons. She told me I should try out for the team. She said, 'We'd love to see you at tryouts.'"

To make the story better, Julia Gillian made the we'd-love-to-see-you-at-tryouts part of the story sound quietly menacing. Bonwit and Cerise looked horrified.

"And Bigfoot was right there," said Julia Gillian. "You know she's a dog hater."

To be honest, Julia Gillian didn't know if this was true, but it seemed as if it could be. Her poor dog. Even though he had been asleep the entire time, she still felt protective of him.

"Did she do anything to him?"

"She laughed at him."

"What did you do?"

"I told her that his name was Tiny."

"You *what?*" said Cerise, looking confused.

It did seem like an odd thing to do, but at least the dog-hating Ms. Caravaggio didn't know Bigfoot's true identity. She was probably up on the eighth-grade floor right now, banging open the bathroom door and thinking that Bigfoot's real name was Tiny.

"Are you thinking of going out for the team?" said Bonwit.

"No way," said Julia Gillian. "I'd be the only

sixth-grader in a bunch of
Sevvies and Crazy
Eights."

She turned around
and looked at the line
of sixth-grade girls
waiting outside the
single-stall gym
bathroom.
It was
a sad
sight.

Mrs. K, the beloved Lake Harriet lunch lady, came tapping by with her dog-head cane. She winked at Julia Gillian.

"How's my true dog person today?" she said.

"Fine, thank you," said Julia Gillian, and winked back at Mrs. K.

Julia Gillian had been practicing her winking for quite some time now, and although it wasn't as effortless as Mrs. K's, there was no telling how good she could get if she just kept practicing and controlling for variables. Maybe all her dreams could come true, including effortless winking, nonstop free throws, and a tour of the world with Bonwit as famous jazz trumpeters. Just then the bell rang, interrupting this pleasant daydream. That meant it was time for reading buddies and Fergus Cannon, who hated to read. Julia Gillian folded her lunch bag in half, then in quarters, then in eighths, and then she got up and trudged to Mr. Lamonte's room.

"Students," said Mr. Lamonte. "Please pay attention. Today's assignment is to look for a book that you will enjoy reading together. And although it might seem too early to talk about, let me remind you that this year's Reading Buddy Extravaganza will be held at the beginning of December, and you and your buddy will soon need to begin working on your project."

Julia Gillian hadn't even thought about the Reading Buddy Extravaganza, which involved the entire media center, a reception for parents and friends, and elaborate projects worked on by the sixth-graders and their reading buddies.

Julia Gillian glanced around Mr. Lamonte's room.

All the other students, it seemed, were chattering happily with their third-grade reading buddies. How was it possible that they had so quickly become so close? Look at Bonwit and Judith Montpelier. Bonwit had brought in a stack of books for Judith to peruse, and Judith was flipping through each one excitedly, as if she had never seen a book before and found them to be extraordinarily interesting. This was a mean thought, but Julia Gillian was envious of Bonwit, who had been paired with such an easy reading buddy.

Cerise, too. Cerise was nodding and smiling and leaning back so far in her chair she looked as if she was about to tip over. Her arms were crossed in front of her chest, and Julia Gillian watched as Mimi Frank, Cerise's

tall reading buddy, now crossed her own arms over her chest. *Monkey see, monkey do*, thought Julia Gillian, which was another mean thought.

She turned back to her own reading buddy. This Fergus Cannon was no piece of cake. His black hair stood up as defiantly as ever, and he had that same flat, determined look in his eyes. Judging from his unblinking stare, she was pretty sure that he had been gazing at her the whole time she glanced about the room. Small as he was, nothing seemed to scare Fergus. She sighed inwardly and took a deep breath.

"I brought in a book for you," said Julia Gillian, trying to sound enthusiastic. "What do you think?"

She pointed at the giant *Collected Plays of William Shakespeare* book sitting on her desk. She had borrowed it from Enzo, who loved William Shakespeare and recommended him to everyone. Julia Gillian suspected that Shakespeare would not be at all appropriate for Fergus Cannon, but she was under orders to bring in a book for her reading buddy, and now she had fulfilled her duty.

Fergus just gave her a disgusted look and pushed at the giant Shakespeare book with the tip of his index finger. It didn't move.

"It's supposed to be good," said Julia Gillian. "Really good."

In her mind she pictured Enzo, who always claimed that William Shakespeare was the greatest writer of all time, living or dead.

"William Shakespeare is the greatest writer of all time, living or dead!" she said.

She tried to put an exclamation mark in her voice, which was the way Mr. Mixler talked, but even to her own ears it sounded false. Fergus didn't even bother to answer. Oh, dear.

"How about the newspaper?" said Julia Gillian. "Do you read the newspaper?"

Newspapers weren't allowed in the reading buddy program — the rules called for books only — but maybe they could make an exception for Fergus Cannon, book-hating third-grader.

"Nope."

"Not even the comics section?"

"Nope."

"How about comic books, then?"

Surely the answer would be yes. Every kid read a comic book at least once in a while.

"Nope."

Fergus Cannon seemed to be capable of a never-ending series of *nopes*. Mr. Mixler, who was passing by in the hall, glanced in and caught sight of Julia Gillian. He grinned his big grin and danced the Mixler Baton through the air. He tipped an imaginary hat in her direction. Oh, if only this were Trumpet class instead of

Reading Buddies. Julia Gillian dragged her eyes back to Fergus Cannon.

"How about music? Do you read music?"

This was grasping at straws, but Julia Gillian was willing to try anything.

"Nope."

Just at that moment, Bonwit and Judith Montpelier burst into delighted laughter. Bonwit grabbed a purple book from the stack and waved it in the air as if it were the Mixler Baton. Judith reached for it, and she and Bonwit staged a mock duel for control of the purple book. It was the battle of the book, and both of them were having fun. Julia Gillian could not imagine ever having any fun with her reading buddy. She still hadn't come up with a single book for Fergus, and everyone else in the class was already working on ideas for the Reading Buddy Extravaganza. Julia Gillian felt a quiet despair.

"Is there *anything* you like?" asked Julia Gillian.

At that, Fergus Cannon sat up straight. Everything about him, including his upright hair, seemed to quiver with love.

"Dogs," he said. "I like dogs."

CHAPTER TEN

By the Grace Nursery Garden Shall We Rest

"Well, at least your reading buddy likes dogs," said Bonwit. "That's a start."

"How is it a start?" said Julia Gillian.

They were walking Bigfoot to the dog park. This was a long walk, far outside Julia Gillian's usual eleven-square-block parameters. But ever since last year, when they had proven themselves to be responsible, their parents had allowed them to walk to the dog park as long as they were together and took the Greenway, which was a trail for pedestrians, bicyclists, and skaters only.

"Because you already have a book about a dog," said

Bonwit. "That green book with the dog on the cover. Remember?"

Remembering was not the problem. Julia Gillian had read that green book two years ago, and she would never forget it. She had begun the green book, which was about a tree house and an old dog and the boy who loved him, in high hopes that she had finally found a book that she could love. But the book had ended sadly, and to this day, Julia Gillian didn't like to think about it. It sat on her bookshelf, and she did not intend to open it again.

"Give him that one to read," said Bonwit encouragingly. "He might love it."

Julia Gillian just shook her head. She didn't want to

talk about the green book. She looked down at her own old dog, who was walking right beside her on his red leash, not that he needed a leash. He had never wanted to be anywhere but right by her side.

"I wish we could still read picture books in sixth grade," said Julia Gillian. "Books are so much better with pictures."

Bonwit nodded, but Julia Gillian knew that he didn't care if a book had pictures or not. That was the difference between a true reader and someone like herself, who preferred a story to be helped along with pictures.

They were passing the Grace Nursery School garden. The children were out, some planting bulbs under

one teacher's supervision, others deadheading the chrysanthemums and raking leaves under the other teacher's supervision. How cute the nursery schoolers were, with their bright sweaters and high voices. A few were running back and forth over the little wooden decorative bridge. Julia Gillian had once been a student at Grace Nursery School, and she always took a proprietary interest in what the children were up to.

Next to her, Bigfoot coughed softly and paused. He always liked observing the children when they were out. Occasionally one of the teachers would offer him a drink from the green garden hose, and he was happy to partake.

"I don't know what to do about my reading buddy," Julia Gillian said. "All he talks about is how much he hates to read. And have you seen that look on his face?"

She gazed at Bonwit with what she hoped was Fergus Cannon's steely, flat look in her eyes. Bonwit looked up and made a face.

"He's not like most third-graders," said Julia Gillian.

"No, he's not," agreed Bonwit.

Julia Gillian distinctly remembered being intimidated by sixth-graders when she was in third grade. She hadn't gone around with a steely, flat look on her face. Even though she didn't like to read, she had been polite to her sixth-grade reading buddy.

The children had now caught sight of Bigfoot, whose tail was wagging gently back and forth. "Bigfoot!

Bigfoot!" they called to him. He had long been a favorite of the nursery school students, who used to call him *Big doggy!* until Julia Gillian had told them his real name.

"Think positively," said Bonwit. "If he's a dog lover, that means there's something good about him."

"That's not going to help when it comes to the Extravaganza project. We can't just paint *I Love Dogs* on the display board, can we?"

Bonwit frowned. No, they couldn't, and he knew it.

"And the Extravaganza is in two months."

"Bigfoot! Bigfoot!"

The children were jumping up and down and singing. Julia Gillian tugged gently on his leash so that they could cross over to the Grace Nursery Garden and let the students pet him. Bigfoot stood still while the children danced about him, holding out their hands to his face. This was not the best way to approach a dog, but they didn't know that. It was a good thing that Bigfoot was so patient.

"Here, let me show you how," said Julia Gillian.

She approached Bigfoot as if she were a stranger, and she held her arm and hand straight down in front of him, so that he could sniff at his leisure and not be frightened, the way many dogs were when strangers tried to pet their heads.

"Good boy," she said soothingly, and the nursery school students imitated her.

At the dog park, Julia Gillian and Bonwit unclipped Bigfoot's leash. He stood by their sides, happily surveying the scene and waving his tail to and fro in the air.

"Look, there's Vince Wintz," said Bonwit.

Vince Wintz was the former lunch monitor at Lake Harriet School, and he and Batman, his three-legged dog, were frequent visitors to the dog park. Although Bonwit and Julia Gillian had gotten off to a rocky start in the lunchroom with Vince, they had come to like him. He was a dog lover and completely devoted to Batman, and that went a long way with Julia Gillian.

"Hello, Batman!" called Bonwit.

Batman, who was only three years old, came galloping over to say hello. Even though he was missing a leg, nothing slowed Batman down. He was a Frisbee dog, which was something else that Julia Gillian admired. He could leap and jump and twirl midair, and he almost always caught the Frisbee unless it landed in the mulberry tree, which happened fairly often. Vince Wintz was not Skilled at the Art of Throwing a Frisbee. Julia Gillian considered suggesting that he control for Frisbee variables.

"Hello, Julia Gillian," said Vince Wintz, who had followed Batman over. "Hello, Bonwit. How are things in the lunchroom these days?"

"Fine," said Julia Gillian.

"Fine," said Bonwit.

They exchanged a swift glance. If truth be told, things were much better than fine in the lunchroom these days, now that Vince Wintz was gone and the beloved Mrs. K was back. Vince Wintz had not allowed them to trade or share food, and he had reported them to their parents if they didn't finish their lunches. Mrs. K did none of those things. But they didn't want to hurt Vince's feelings, so they said nothing.

"And how are you these days, Bigfoot?"

They all looked at Bigfoot, who was still standing by Julia Gillian's side. He hadn't even ventured forth to walk the perimeter of the park, as had long been his habit. But now he looked up and hung out his tongue and wagged his tail.

CHAPTER ELEVEN

The Big Heart of the St. Bernard

The Uptown Vet was a familiar place to Julia Gillian and her parents. Dr. Gowdy had been giving Bigfoot his annual check-ups ever since he was a puppy. Now Julia Gillian and her parents sat in the waiting room, next to the large bowl of water that all dogs were welcome to drink from. The rock fountain in the little alcove splashed steadily, the way it always did, and the big container of dog treats sat on the counter in the same place. The Uptown Vet smelled comfortingly of dogs and dog treats and lavender and pine.

Dr. Gowdy poked her head out of the room where

she and her assistant had taken Bigfoot. This was a routine visit, but when she heard his little cough, Dr. Gowdy had given him an X-ray. She was a conscientious doctor who wanted to make sure she had thought of everything.

"You can come back with me now," said Dr. Gowdy.

In the back room, Bigfoot sat by the window. He looked up when they came into the room and thumped his tail twice. *There you are, Dog of My Dreams*, beamed Julia Gillian to him telepathically.

An X-ray was up on the computer screen, and Julia Gillian looked at it. The X-ray must be a picture of the inside of Bigfoot, but she was not a doctor, and she didn't know how to read X-rays.

"How long has Bigfoot had his little cough?" said Dr. Gowdy.

"Since school started," said Julia Gillian.

Dr. Gowdy nodded thoughtfully.

"Let me tell you what's happening," she said.

Dr. Gowdy sat on the metal examining table. When Bigfoot was younger, he had sat up there, too. Julia Gillian used to put her arms around him to help hold him steady when he got his vaccinations. When he was bigger, the assistant had put a stepstool at the foot of the table, and he had climbed right up onto it when Julia Gillian said, "Up, Bigfoot." Bigfoot had always been a good and obedient dog.

"Bigfoot is an old dog now," said Dr. Gowdy.

Yes, he is an old dog, thought Julia Gillian. *So what*? She stroked him behind the ears, especially behind his right ear, which was his favorite. Her parents were sitting in chairs on either side of Bigfoot, each with a hand on his back.

"He's especially old for a St. Bernard."

No one said anything. Julia Gillian waited for Dr. Gowdy to take out her prescription pad and write a prescription for some pills that would get rid of the cough. Julia Gillian knew how to give a dog a pill so that he swallowed it right down. You could say that she was highly Skilled at the Art of Pilling a Dog.

"Dogs like Bigfoot often develop health problems when they get old. Some of those problems include hip dysplasia, which makes it hard for them to walk."

That didn't sound so bad. If walking was the problem, Julia Gillian would walk very slowly and let Bigfoot take his time. Maybe her mother and father could hook up a trailer to her bike, and then she could pedal around the lake with Bigfoot sitting in the trailer. That would be fun.

"Bigfoot doesn't have hip dysplasia, which is good," said Dr. Gowdy. "But he does have something called cardiomyopathy, which is a kind of heart disease."

She pointed at the light box. None of them could understand the X-ray, but they all stared at it anyway.

"Bigfoot's heart is enlarged, and it's gotten hard for it to pump blood throughout his body."

She tapped her finger on the X-ray, but it just looked like a cloudy shadow to Julia Gillian. How could anyone make sense of such a thing?

"A normal heart would be half this size," said Dr. Gowdy.

Of course Bigfoot's heart is big, thought Julia Gillian. *He is a loyal and loving and devoted dog.*

Dr. Gowdy turned to look at the X-ray again. She looked at it for quite a long time, and when she turned around again, her eyes were wet.

"A little cough is one of the symptoms of cardiomyopathy," she said. "Bigfoot's heart is failing. I'm so sorry."

Julia Gillian could hear her parents asking questions and Dr. Gowdy answering, but she couldn't make out what exactly they were saying. *Bigfoot's heart is failing.* Those were the words she kept hearing, as if Dr. Gowdy were saying them over and over. She stood beside her dog, stroking the soft back of his right ear over and over. His tail swept slowly back and forth across the floor.

Bigfoot's skinny brown bat was on the windowsill. *Bigfoot needs his bat*, thought Julia Gillian, and she picked it up and held it out to Bigfoot, who took it between his jaws.

"His heart is big," said Julia Gillian. "It's *big*. That's all."

It seemed important to make her parents and the doctor understand that a big heart was a good thing. Dr. Gowdy came over and knelt beside her.

Julia Gillian stared at her.

"You mean you're not going to do anything?"

"There's nothing to do, honey. His heart has to work too hard," said Dr. Gowdy. "There isn't any medicine that will help him. I'm so sorry, Julia Gillian."

Julia Gillian disliked it when anyone but her parents called her *honey*. She kept stroking the fur behind Bigfoot's ears. Her parents and Dr. Gowdy were silent.

"Well, someone has to do something," she said.

No one said anything. Julia Gillian looked at them

again. Julia Gillian's mother was pressing her fingers on her eyes the way she did when she was trying not to cry. Her father was still staring at the X-ray. What was wrong with them all?

"Someone has to do something," Julia Gillian said again.

Still no one said anything.

Long ago, Julia Gillian and her parents had talked about what they would do if Bigfoot ever got very old and very sick. They had decided that they would not want to see him suffer, and that if that time ever came, they would want him to go peacefully. But that discussion had been long ago — years and years ago, when Bigfoot was a young dog — and the possibility of him getting old and sick had not seemed real to

Julia Gillian. It still didn't seem real to her. She refused to think about the possibility.

If no one else was going to do anything, she would.

"Honey, Bigfoot will keep slowing down," said Dr. Gowdy. "He'll sleep more often and for longer periods of time."

Honey. There it was again.

"We can control for variables," said Julia Gillian, ignoring what Dr. Gowdy was saying. "That's what we can do."

Someone had to do something, and if it had to be Julia Gillian, then fine, she would do it. She would not give up. She would make a list of Bigfoot variables, and she would control for them. In this way, she would keep her dog safe.

CHAPTER TWELVE

The Bigfoot Variables

When they brought him back from the Uptown Vet, Bigfoot climbed the stairs to their apartment. Slowly, but still, he had climbed them without help. And once inside, he made his way to the kitchen, where he lapped up half the water in his bowl. And then he lay down on his long magenta cushion, positioned his bat underneath his paw, and fell right to sleep. Julia Gillian sat on her bed for a while, watching his chest rise and fall with each breath, and then she went out to the living room. Her parents were sitting on the couch, looking at the coffee table.

"I'm going to Bonwit's house," she said.

They looked up at her and nodded. There was no

reason to tell them why she was going to Bonwit's; they knew that she needed to tell her best friend the news of Bigfoot's enlarged heart. Julia Gillian walked the familiar blocks to Bonwit's house, where they sat together in his room, with the Tiny Tornadoes screaming downstairs, for a long time. When she came home, her parents were still sitting on the couch, looking at the coffee table. The silence was unbearable.

She decided to practice her free throws.

It was dark out. But the alley streetlights were on, and Julia Gillian could still see her basketball and the rim of the hoop just fine. Fine enough to keep practicing. Fine enough to keep controlling for free-throw variables. Not that it was working tonight.

Basket —

— *ball.*

Bounce. Bounce. Bounce.

Crouch and fling.

Bang. Once again the basketball hit the wrong part of the backboard and bounced off down the alley. Julia Gillian glanced at her apartment building, where all the windows were brightly lit. She looked up at her own apartment, where she could see her mother and father still sitting in the living room. She looked at the floor directly below, where once in a while she could see Enzo or Zap passing through their own living room.

Basket —

— *ball.*

Bounce. Bounce. Bounce.

Crouch and fling.

Bang. She had not made a single basket. Controlling for variables must be harder at night, although the only thing truly different, as far as she could see, was the lack of sunlight. She looked back at her apartment, at her bedroom window, which was also brightly lit. Was Bigfoot still asleep in there, on his long magenta cushion?

Basket —

— *ball.*

Bounce. Bounce. Bounce.

Crouch and fling.

Bang.

"Oops," said a voice. "Here you go."

Julia Gillian turned to see Ms. Caravaggio standing by her bike in the shadows by the garage on the other side of the alley. Was she a ghost girl, traveling through the alleys in the middle of the night? It wasn't the middle of the night — it wasn't even Julia Gillian's bedtime   but still. She bounced the ball back to Julia Gillian.

Julia Gillian said nothing. She positioned herself exactly in place and tried to ignore the presence of Ms. Caravaggio, which was hard, seeing as both her hair and the spokes of her bike were glimmering in the streetlight.

Basket —

— ball.

Bounce. Bounce. Bounce.

Crouch and fling.

Bang.

"Not a good night for free throws," said Ms. Caravaggio.

She hopped off her bike and retrieved the ball. She stood still for a moment, and then suddenly, Ms. Caravaggio was dribbling toward the basket. Her cloud of blond hair floated behind her, waving up and down.

"Let's try some layups," she called.

Layups? The only experience that Julia Gillian had with layups was when she played MEERKAT with her parents.

There went Ms. Caravaggio. Dribble, dribble, dribble, and suddenly she was hunched over and pounding toward the basket, and then she was leaping up with a quick midair twirl, and the ball slipped right into the basket.

"Your turn!" called Ms. Caravaggio, and bounce-passed the ball to Julia Gillian, who caught it before she could think.

Dribble. Dribble. Dribble. Dribble. Dribble. Dribble. Crouch and leap and —

Thunk.

Oh, dear. How had Ms. Caravaggio made it look so easy? If only she had asked for free throws instead of layups. After all, Julia Gillian had been controlling for free-throw variables for months now.

"Good try," said Ms. Caravaggio. "Do you want to play some one-on-one?"

Julia Gillian shook her head. She reminded herself that she wanted nothing to do with this eighth-grader.

"Where's your dog, Tiny?"

"He's upstairs, resting," said Julia Gillian. "He's eleven. That's old for a St. Bernard."

She hadn't intended to say anything, but she had. Now Ms. Caravaggio knew something real about Bigfoot, something truly personal.

"He has a big heart," said Julia Gillian.

What was wrong with her? *Just keep quiet,* she told herself. She wanted this mean, dog-hating girl to leave. But Ms. Caravaggio didn't leave.

Ms. Caravaggio said nothing. She swung her leg over her bike and put one foot up on a pedal, tilting slightly back and forth to keep her balance.

"I'm going to be controlling for variables for him from now on," said Julia Gillian.

Just. Shut. Up, Julia Gillian scolded herself.

"Good-bye," she said, and she turned toward her apartment building.

"From now on, my dear dog, we're going to be controlling for your variables," Julia Gillian said to Bigfoot.

Actually, it was she who would be controlling for variables, but she didn't want Bigfoot to feel left out, so she used the royal *we*. That was what Enzo had told her it was called, and Enzo knew her words, not to mention her Shakespeare. Bigfoot thumped his tail. He was resting on his long magenta pillow, his bat tucked under his jaw.

"For one thing, no more long walks," said Julia Gillian. "Too tiring."

Bigfoot tilted his head. This meant he was listening carefully, even if he didn't understand exactly what Julia Gillian was saying.

"For another thing, plenty of rest."

Julia Gillian decided to make a formal list. She took out an old math challenge sheet and made notes with her nearly new brown Sharpie on the back of it.

**CONTROLLING
FOR BIGFOOT
VARIABLES**

1. NO LONG WALKS
   (TOO TIRING)

2. PLENTY OF SLEEP
   (TO REST THE HEART)

She looked over her list. Was there anything she was leaving out? Dr. Gowdy had said that there was nothing to be done for Bigfoot's enlarged heart, but Julia Gillian refused to believe that was true. She thought carefully. What about his stuffed bat? Most of the time, Bigfoot carried it around in his mouth, but once in a while he liked to shake it back and forth wildly. That could not be good for his heart, and Julia Gillian decided to call a halt to it immediately.

3. NO SHAKING OF BAT
   (TOO STRENUOUS)

"No more bat shaking," said Julia Gillian to Bigfoot.

He tilted his head in the other direction and, as if he understood what she was saying, placed his paw over the skinny stuffed brown bat. Julia Gillian remembered the day she had won that bat in the claw machine. She had been trying to win a stuffed meerkat, but instead, the skinny bat had dropped into the chute. While she had been terribly disappointed, she had to admit that the bat had made Bigfoot

very happy. Still, one

couldn't

be too

careful.

CHAPTER THIRTEEN

Is That a Sad Book?

"Pay attention, sixth-graders," said Mr. Lamonte. "Reading Buddy Extravaganza is in six short weeks, and you are expected to do a superlative job on your projects."

He swept the room with a Lamonte Look, but no one was intimidated. They were all used to the Lamonte Look by now.

"My classes always perform well at the Extravaganza, and this year should be no exception. How many of you have decided on your project topic?"

Hands shot up. Bonwit's and Judith Montpelier's hands wiggled in the air. That was how happy they were with their project topic, which, given their mutual interest in scary books, suited them both: "Various and Sundry Nights of Fright." They had compromised on their title. Bonwit had come up with the phrase "Various and Sundry Creatures," and Judith, who liked rhymes, had added "Nights of Fright."

Bonwit was good at writing, and Judith was good at rhyming, and they were both good at drawing. They were planning to write illustrated book reports of the seven frightening books they had read together as reading buddies. Seven! Julia Gillian mentally shook her head at the very thought of seven books. She and Fergus had not even started one.

Now Bonwit turned to Julia Gillian.

"Do you and Fergus want to come over to my house this Saturday to work on your project? Judith will be there."

Of course Judith would be there, enjoying herself amid the pots of paint and colored paper and many art supplies lining the shelves and table of Bonwit's dining room.

"Francine and Georgia will probably be screaming," said Bonwit, "but you're welcome anyway."

Julia Gillian gave him a look. She knew he was trying to encourage her in her reading buddy project, but the truth was that she and Fergus had made no headway at all. He had rejected all her suggestions, and she felt a growing sense of hopelessness. She had tried, but what could you do with a third-grader who flatly refused to try any book at all? At Bonwit's suggestion, she had even brought in the green book with the dog on the cover, but Fergus had given her a suspicious look.

"Is that a sad book?" he said. "Tell me the truth."

Julia Gillian shrugged. She didn't want to discourage Fergus, but she couldn't deny that the green book

was indeed sad. She could hardly stand to think about it, in fact, especially since she had learned about Bigfoot's heart condition. Even though she was determined to control for all Bigfoot variables, she kept thinking about what Dr. Gowdy had said. *Bigfoot will keep slowing down.*

"Does the dog die in the end?"

At this, Bonwit, who had overheard, shot Julia Gillian a worried look. He knew how sad she was feeling, even though she tried to hide it. Julia Gillian had hesitated, then nodded. At that, Fergus shook his head, a quick, definitive back and forth.

"Nope," he said, and that was that.

The low buzz of conversation rose around the room as Julia Gillian's friends turned to their reading buddies to continue work on their projects. She looked at Fergus, who was looking straight at her with his usual flat, determined look. His hair was sticking straight up, the way it always did, but Julia Gillian no longer bothered to wonder how it stayed that way. Bonwit and Judith were chattering away as they sketched out a preliminary design for their Nights of Fright project. Mimi was pointing at Cerise and laughing so hard that she made no sound, while Cerise leaned back in her chair smiling, proud that she had said something so funny.

Julia Gillian got up from her seat and went up to Mr. Lamonte, who looked up from his grade book.

"Mr. Lamonte, I have a problem. My reading buddy hates to read."

"Surely he doesn't hate to read everything."

"He does, though."

Julia Gillian gestured behind
her, so that Mr. Lamonte
could observe for himself
Fergus Cannon's steely
look of book hatred.

"What books have you suggested to him?"

"A green one," said Julia Gillian. "But he wouldn't even look at it."

"Surely you didn't give up at just one book. What else have you tried?"

"The Collected Plays of William Shakespeare."

Mr. Lamonte looked surprised.

"My neighbor Enzo thought that he might like it," said Julia Gillian. "She says that Shakespeare is the greatest writer of all time, living or dead."

"That may well be," said Mr. Lamonte. "But I suggest that you focus on your reading buddy's personal interests. What does he like, for example?"

"Dogs," said Julia Gillian.

Mr. Lamonte nodded briskly, as if the problem were solved.

"There you go then," he said. "Dogs it is."

Dogs it wasn't, thought Julia Gillian. She had already proved that with the green book. Mr. Lamonte did not understand the depth of the problem. She trudged back to her desk, where Fergus Cannon was removing the pencil-top eraser from his stub of a pencil and putting

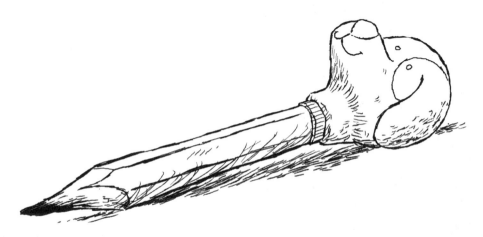

it back on. Remove, replace. Remove, replace. His pencil-top eraser was in the shape of a dog, she noticed. A beagle, to be exact.

"Is your own dog a beagle?" she said.

They still had half an hour left. She might as well keep trying to make conversation.

"I don't have a dog."

"But I thought you loved dogs."

"I do."

"Then why don't you have one?"

Fergus Cannon removed his beagle eraser and replaced it. Remove, replace.

"Because they don't allow them in my apartment building," he said.

"Oh no," said Julia Gillian.

As difficult as Fergus Cannon was, Julia Gillian felt a rush of sympathy for him. How terrible to love dogs but not be able to have one.

"I have to wait until I'm grown up and living on my own before I can have a dog," said Fergus Cannon.

"Well, that won't be so long," said Julia Gillian.

She was only trying to help, but he gave her a look of deep scorn and returned to his pencil stub and its beagle eraser. Remove, replace. Remove, replace. The truth was that it would be at least ten years before Fergus could have a dog of his own, and that was indeed a long time. Fergus was not the kind of third-grader who would go along with false comfort.

"I have a dog," she said.

Now he looked up.

"You do?"

"He's a St. Bernard."

"What's his name?"

"Bigfoot."

Julia Gillian hesitated, then removed her precious photo of Bigfoot from the front pouch of her backpack, where she carried it always. It was her favorite photo of

him, taken when he was just a puppy, sitting on his long magenta pillow with his red leash in his mouth. This was the photo that she had shown Bonwit, way back in kindergarten. This was the photo that had cemented their friendship. It was old and faded now, but Julia Gillian treasured it.

Fergus laid his beagle eraser on the desk and leaned forward. His eyes were alight with interest.

"How old is he now?"

"Old."

The lump rose in Julia Gillian's throat again. This happened every time she thought about her dog these days. Fergus was looking at her.

"Really old?"

Julia Gillian nodded. It was all she could do. Fergus picked up his beagle-eraser pencil and opened his notebook. He began to sketch something on a blank page while she tried to swallow past the lump in her throat. His pencil flew, and as she watched, a dog took shape on the page. It was a St. Bernard, shaggy, with a dignified head and deep, intelligent eyes.

"Does your dog look like this?" said Fergus.

Julia Gillian nodded. That was indeed what her dog looked like.

"He has an extra-big heart," she said. "But I'm controlling for variables, and he'll be just fine."

Fergus could have no idea what she was talking about, but he was preoccupied anyway, shading in

the paws on the St. Bernard. Then, in fancy letters,
he wrote *Bigfoot* underneath his sketch, and circled
it with a wavy dark line. He tilted his head and
studied the drawing without saying anything. That
was the way it was with artists. Julia Gillian had
often observed this same behavior in Bonwit's

mother, who, before Francine and Georgia were born, used to focus so intently on her paintings that she sometimes didn't hear what Bonwit or Julia Gillian was saying. Now Fergus frowned, as if her words had just filtered in.

"What does 'controlling for variables' mean?"

"It means that I'm going to keep Bigfoot safe," said Julia Gillian.

Fergus drew a heart on the St. Bernard, a heart so large that it filled up his entire chest. This was a remarkable drawing. Fergus might not be a reader, but he was a truly talented artist. *My third-grade reading buddy has drawn a beautiful picture of you*, she beamed telepathically to Bigfoot, safe at home in their apartment.

CHAPTER FOURTEEN
Keeping Him Safe

"Hello, Dog of My Dreams," said Julia Gillian.

As always, Bigfoot was waiting for her just inside the door to the apartment. As always, his tail was brushing back and forth across the floor. He tilted his head and looked up at her with his brown eyes.

"You certainly may have a treat," she said, responding to his telepathically beamed question.

Both Bigfoot and Bonwit understood Julia Gillian's telepathically beamed thoughts, and she understood theirs. That was the thing about best friends.

In the kitchen, Julia Gillian chose a special Zap treat, a homemade salmon-and-sweet-potato dog biscuit in the shape of a star. Zap had invented these treats two

years ago, when he was a beginning
student at the Dunwoody
Culinary Institute, and he
called them Bigfoot Wows.
They were a hit with all
manner of dogs, Bigfoot
especially.

Bigfoot crunched down his Bigfoot Wow and tilted
his head again. That meant that he was asking if they
could go on their long walk now, as was their routine.

"I'm sorry, Bigfoot," said Julia Gillian. "But there will
be no more long walks."

She took her Controlling for Bigfoot Variables list
out of her backpack and pointed at #1.

"Too tiring," she said. "Not good for your heart."

Bigfoot wagged his tail. He walked to the door, where his red leash hung from its hook, and looked up at it inquiringly.

"If you're worried about going to the bathroom," said Julia Gillian, "don't. Of course we'll be going outside for that."

She took down the leash and clipped it to his collar. This would be an adjustment for her as well, because she and Bigfoot were used to taking an eleven-square-block walk every afternoon. But her goal was to keep Bigfoot strong and healthy, and if that meant plenty of rest, then so be it.

Down the hall they went. At the bottom of the first set of stairs, Bigfoot looked down the hall in the direction of Zap and Enzo's apartment.

"You want to go visit Enzo?" said Julia Gillian. "Okay. Right after we go outside."

After he peed, Bigfoot started down Emerson at a brisk pace, as was his custom when beginning their daily long walk. Julia Gillian pulled back on the leash.

"No, no," she said. "No more long walks for us."

Bigfoot paused and looked back at her. He was clearly puzzled. Why were they not heading down Emerson, and then on to 36th Street, and over to Bryant Hardware, and, since it was such a nice day, down to Lake Calhoun, where they could admire the windsurfers and the children swinging on the playground?

"Too tiring," said Julia Gillian.

She patted her heart, as if to remind him that his own heart was enlarged. He turned his head back in

the direction of their walk and swept his tail very slowly
once through the air. Julia Gillian felt the same way
as Bigfoot. Giving up their daily walk was not going to
be easy.

"But guess what?" she said, trying to make her voice
sound light and happy. "Now we can go visit Enzo."

Bigfoot tilted his head. Bigfoot and Julia Gillian were used to communicating honestly on all levels, and even to her own ears, her voice sounded false.

"Yes, it's Enzo time."

What was she doing, saying *Yes, it's Enzo time?* That was completely unlike her. These new Bigfoot variable rules would take some getting used to.

KNOCK. KNOCK. KNOCK.

KnockKnockKnock.

Knock. Knock. Knock.

"Noodlie!"

Enzo flung open the door. She was wearing her platform army shoes today, which made her quite a bit taller than Julia Gillian.

"And Bigfoot! Come in, favorite neighbors. Come in and rest your weary bones."

This was one of Enzo's favorite sayings. Julia Gillian sat down on the hammock, and Bigfoot stretched out underneath the living room window. Enzo sat cross-legged in her brown velvet chair.

"Why aren't you on your long walk?" said Enzo. "It's that time of day, isn't it?"

"No more long walks," said Julia Gillian. "Too tiring."

She looked over at Bigfoot and put her hand on her heart. Enzo responded by putting her own hand on her own heart, but she was clearly confused.

"Bigfoot has an enlarged heart," said Julia Gillian. "It's called cardiomyopathy."

Enzo kept her hand on her heart and looked sharply at Julia Gillian. Julia Gillian's father had long said that Enzo had a mind like a steel trap. Now she sat very still in her brown velvet chair, and Julia Gillian could tell that she was trying to figure out what was going on.

"What does that mean for Bigfoot, exactly?"

"It means that we need to keep him safe," said Julia Gillian. "It means that we have to control for enlarged heart variables."

She pulled the Controlling for Bigfoot Variables list out of her back pocket and handed it to Enzo. It was a short list, but Enzo took her time studying it.

"I see," said Enzo. "So, this is the way it is from now on?"

Julia Gillian nodded.

"No long walks, plenty of sleep, and no shaking of bat."

Julia Gillian nodded again. They both looked over at Bigfoot, whose head was resting on his front paws.

"Does Bigfoot like the new rules?" said Enzo.

"He has to get used to them."

"Do you like the new rules?"

"I have to get used to them, too."

Enzo uncrossed her legs and stood up. She picked up *The Collected Plays of William Shakespeare*, which was an extremely large book, and placed it on her head. She walked back and forth in front of the hammock a few times, with her arms held out for balance. Enzo was a believer in excellent posture, and she said that walking with a heavy book on your head was a good way to practice.

"I don't know, Noodlie," she said after a while. "I don't know if these new rules are such a good idea." It was unlike Enzo, who usually did not question Julia Gillian's decisions, to say something like this. Julia Gillian looked at her closely.

"Bigfoot is an old dog," Enzo said. "Not in human years, but in dog years. And — "

"I know he's an old dog! Stop telling me he's an old dog!"

Enzo stood still, with William Shakespeare balanced on her head, and looked straight back at Julia Gillian, who kept on yelling.

"Everyone keeps saying he's an old dog! I'm sick of it! Sick, sick, sick of it!"

It was only when Bigfoot hauled himself to his feet, came over to the hammock, and pushed his nose into her hand that she realized she was upsetting him. A dog with an enlarged heart should not be subjected to yelling like this. Julia Gillian stopped. No more yelling, she thought. Too upsetting.

"I'm sorry, Noodlie," said Enzo.

"There's nothing to be sorry about," said Julia Gillian. "Bigfoot is going to be fine."

CHAPTER FIFTEEN

What Kind of a Book
Has No Pictures?

"How's it going with the free-throw variables?" said Bonwit at lunch.

"Good."

"What are you up to now?" said Lathrop, who was listening in.

"One hundred forty-four."

Julia Gillian said this modestly, but the truth was that she was proud of having surpassed her previous record by so much. That was the beauty of controlling for variables.

"And how's it going with the Bigfoot variables?" said Bonwit.

"Not very well," said Julia Gillian.

If anyone else had asked, she would have tried to sound positive and upbeat, but Bonwit was her best friend, and there was no need to keep secrets from him. She looked down at her cream cheese and jelly sandwich. The tiny lunch note of the day read *Have a happy day, honey.* This was a pretty unoriginal note, but still, Julia Gillian was glad to have it. It was nice to know that her parents were thinking about her. As long as it was her parents, she didn't mind being called *honey*.

"Does he miss his long walks?"

"We both do."

There was a hole in the afternoon now, a hole that used to be nicely filled with a long, eleven-square-block walk. Julia Gillian missed walking by the kind Girard

Avenue person's house with the water bowl out front and the laminated sign that read DOGS! PLEASE HELP YOURSELVES!, and she missed going to the dog park, where she could admire the other dogs and sometimes see Vince Wintz and three-legged Batman. She missed walking to Bryant Hardware with Bigfoot, so that they could stand in front of the display window and admire the seasonal decorations. Right now, for example, all

the Halloween decorations were up — the witch with the warty nose, the scary masks — and Bigfoot had not even seen them. Julia Gillian knew that Bigfoot missed his routine, too. He still waited by the door every afternoon, pushing at his red leash with his nose and looking up at her.

"Is he getting lots of extra sleep?" said Bonwit.

Julia Gillian shook her head. She encouraged Bigfoot

to take naps, but he was not the sort of dog who could sleep on demand. Julia Gillian lay down on her own bed each afternoon and closed her eyes, in order to set a good example, but it turned out that she was not the kind of girl who could sleep on demand, either.

"What about his bat?" said Bonwit.

"Up on a high shelf," said Julia Gillian. "Next to the green book."

"Do you think he likes the new rules?"

"No."

Bonwit nodded. This was as he had expected. But if Bigfoot was going to remain safe from the dangers of his enlarged heart, there could be no going back to the old, lazy ways.

"Did you finish your Tiny Tornado list?" she said.

Bonwit, living in the midst of the frequent chaos that had become his family's life since Francine and Georgia were born, had also decided to make a list. The Controlling for Tiny Tornado Variables list was more extensive than the Bigfoot list. Now he pulled it out of his back pocket and spread it on the lunch table.

1. Mobiles on at all times and plenty of toys nearby (to distract them).

2. Make sure diapers are clean and dry (parents only)

3. Turn on fan when napping (white noise)

4. Pay equal attention to each Tornado (to avoid jealousy).

The list went on and on, and Julia Gillian felt a little tired, reading it. It seemed as if Bonwit was trying to control for *all* possible variables. She could understand this — when the Tiny Tornadoes were unhappy, everyone in the Keller house was unhappy — but still, it seemed like a great deal of work.

"How's it going?" she said.

Bonwit shook his head. "It's hard. The Tornadoes don't even try. I think they *like* to scream."

"Maybe it'll get better when they're older."

Julia Gillian privately didn't hold out much hope that Francine and Georgia would improve much — they did seem to enjoy screaming more than anything else — but she didn't want to sound discouraging. At least Bonwit was lucky in that the Tornadoes were human. He didn't have to worry about their hearts enlarging in just a few years.

It was fundamentally unfair that dogs aged so much faster than humans, but nevertheless, Julia Gillian was determined to beat the odds. She pictured Bigfoot, home in the apartment, and sent him a telepathic scratch behind the ears. Maybe he was taking a nap. Maybe he was getting used to the new rules. She hoped he wasn't gazing longingly at his bat, up there on the high shelf next to the green book.

Three aisles away, Mrs. K winked at Julia Gillian. *How's my true dog person?*, she mouthed. Julia Gillian was skilled at the art of reading Mrs. K's lips, and she mouthed, *Fine*, and winked back. She wasn't really fine, but there was no sense getting into the Bigfoot variables list with Mrs. K just as lunch was ending. Mrs. K raised her dog-head cane in the air and shook it. That meant *Solidarity,* which was one of Mrs. K's favorite expressions.

"Time for Reading Buddies," said Bonwit.

He sounded happy, which made sense, since he and Judith Montpelier got along so well.

"Oh, great," said Julia Gillian. "Just great."

She made her way down the hall to Mr. Lamonte's classroom with Bonwit, dawdling to the extent possible. Another hour with Fergus Cannon, who after six weeks still refused to read any of the dog books she suggested — *Dog Cartoons Throughout the Ages,* for example, or *Dog Heroes of the Civil War* — was just what she didn't need. The third-grade buddies began filing in, and the sight of them made Julia Gillian feel even worse.

How happy they all looked, these little third-graders. And why wouldn't they? They had a bathroom in their very own classroom. They never had to venture up the dreaded eighth-grade stairs to use the lone middle school bathroom. Their lives were simple and secure.

And how happy her friends looked with them. There was Cerise with her buddy, Mimi Frank, for example. They were doing a collage of Amelia Earhart, American aviator, who, as it happened, was a hero to both of them. Today Mimi was wearing black-and-white polka-dot gloves that came up to her elbows. Julia Gillian had never seen gloves like these. They were dizzying. She wondered if they made writing difficult.

And Bonwit and Judith Montpelier were actually high-fiving each other. Maybe that was because they were nearly finished with their "Various and Sundry Nights of Fright" project. Did these two never tire of reading? Did they never want to just put down their

books, clip a leash to a dog, and take him on an extra-long walk? Julia Gillian wished fiercely that she could leave Reading Buddies, right at this moment, and take Bigfoot on an extra-long walk. But no, she must stay here and wait for Fergus Cannon, who usually straggled in after the rest of his class. She had gotten a very bad deal.

Bonwit broke away from Judith Montpelier, who was applying glitter glue to one of the Nights of Fright creatures on their poster board, and gave her a sympathetic look. He knew how she felt about her reading buddy.

"Maybe you should control for variables with Fergus," said Bonwit. "Think about it. What can you rule out in order to focus on a good outcome?"

"Everything," said Julia Gillian. "Everything in the world, except dogs."

For some reason, this remark struck both her and Bonwit as extremely funny. When Bonwit laughed hard, his entire face squinched tight, his body shook up and down instead of sideways, and instead of a typical laugh, he made a strange sighing sound. How Julia Gillian loved to see Bonwit laugh like this. Just then, Fergus came trudging in. For a moment, she pictured

him as the smushable third-grader of Principal Smartt's annual stairs lecture, mashed against the wall by a stampeding herd of tall, loud eighth-graders, led by Ms. Caravaggio.

"What's so funny?" said Fergus Cannon, giving them his flat-eyed look.

"Why, not a thing, Mr. Cannon," said Bonwit.

This was so unlike Bonwit that Julia Gillian snorted

in surprise. It was good to laugh, and she wanted to keep on laughing, but there was tiny Fergus, who was not laughing at all.

"I read a book," said Fergus. "Are you happy?"

This was such unexpected news that Bonwit and Julia Gillian both stopped laughing immediately.

"You read a book?" said Julia Gillian. "What book?"

"Some book. I can't remember what it was. There was an old guy in it."

"Was it any good?"

Fergus grimaced and shook his head. You had to admire him for those looks of his, thought Julia Gillian. Only a third-grader, but unafraid, and always honest.

"Why not?" ventured Bonwit, who had rarely met a book he didn't like.

Fergus gave him a look of deep scorn.

"No pictures. What kind of a book has no pictures?"

So true, thought Julia Gillian. She looked at him in surprise. For once they were on the same footing, and it didn't have to do with dogs. In Julia Gillian's opinion, books should contain pictures, and lots of them, and it was apparent that Fergus felt the same way.

And just then, Julia Gillian got an idea for a Reading Buddy Extravaganza project. Her idea was unorthodox, but then, so was Fergus.

"Fergus," she said. "Why don't we write our own book for the Extravaganza?"

CHAPTER SIXTEEN
What's the Worst that Can Happen?

"Will they let us?" said Fergus. "Will they let us write our own book?"

"I don't know," Julia Gillian said.

And she didn't. All the other reading buddy projects consisted of variations on book reports. A book report was the tried and true traditional Reading Buddy Extravaganza project, but Julia Gillian had always hated writing book reports.

"They probably won't," said Fergus. "They never let us do anything fun."

This was not true — Julia Gillian had plenty of fun in school — but now that she and Fergus had found common ground, she didn't want to start disagreeing again.

"Let's just go ahead and start," said Julia Gillian. "What's the worst that can happen?"

The worst that could happen, she supposed, was that their project would be disallowed. Then they would have to start over and do a traditional book report project. But if that was the worst, Julia Gillian could live with it.

"What should our book be about?" she said.

"Dogs. Duh."

Such scorn. Was this boy ever intimidated?

"Bonwit, may I borrow your red Sharpie?" said Julia Gillian.

Bonwit handed her his red Sharpie. Julia Gillian

was very fond of her brown Sharpie, but red seemed like a better choice than brown for her and Fergus's book. Red was cheerful, and Julia Gillian wanted to write a cheerful book about happiness. In her opinion, too many books were sad. Take the green book on her high shelf, for example.

"You write," said Fergus. "I'll draw."

This was a command, and Julia Gillian ordinarily refused to obey commands without a *please* attached, but this time she didn't argue. She, too, was eager to get going. This was just the kind of project she liked — something she could make up herself and work on until it was good. It was the reason she so enjoyed making papier-mâché masks. She ripped a sheet of paper out of her notebook and set to work.

A
CHEERFUL
BOOK

BY JULIA GILLIAN
AND FERGUS CANNON

Obviously, this was a temporary title, but Julia Gillian felt that they needed a title, even a temporary one, to get started on the book. It was a little intimidating, looking at all the lines on this piece of paper. How should she begin? She knew how to begin making a papier-mâché mask — picture it in her head, and then start in with the newspaper strips and paste — but she'd never tried to write a book before.

Fergus was already hard at work, drawing the head of a dog. She was happy to see that it was a St. Bernard.

Julia Gillian looked over at Bonwit and Judith

Montpelier, laughing away. If asked, they would no doubt have a million ideas for a cheerful book, even though it would probably be a book about cheerful, scary creatures of the nighttime.

She looked over at Cerise and Mimi Frank, who were both leaning back in their chairs the way they had been told over and over not to do. Mimi was gesturing animatedly. Her long black-and-white polka-dot gloves moved back and forth in the air. It made Julia Gillian a bit queasy to look at them, so she looked down at her sheet of notebook paper.

If only she could be home right now, clipping the red leash to Bigfoot's collar, heading down Emerson on a long, long walk.

> If only I could be home
> right now, the girl thought.
> If only I could be home,
> clipping the red leash to
> my dog's collar, ready to
> head on our long daily
> walk.

There. That sentence alone had taken up seven whole

lines of notebook paper. Julia Gillian was impressed. It

wasn't all that cheerful of a sentence, though. She decided

to try again.

> What a cheerful, cheerful
> day thought the girl.
> Soon she would be home,
> clipping the red leash to
> her dogs collar, ready
> to head out on their
> long, daily walk.

That was much better. It was a cheerful day in a cheerful book, and a girl was about to take her dog on a long walk. What should the dog look like? And what should his name be?

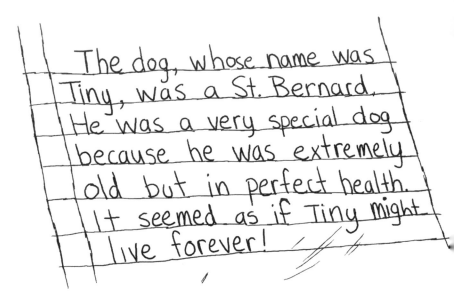

The dog, whose name was Tiny, was a St. Bernard. He was a very special dog because he was extremely old but in perfect health. It seemed as if Tiny might live forever!

That was the most cheerful sentence Julia Gillian had ever seen, and she had to stop to admire it. *It seemed as if Tiny might live forever!* She had already filled up half the page, and it hadn't been difficult at all. In the seat next to her, Fergus had finished the outline of the St. Bernard and was drawing a happy expression on his face. Julia Gillian was happy to see that Fergus, too, seemed to have the same cheerful-book goal that she did.

CHAPTER SEVENTEEN

So Many Variables

At recess, Julia Gillian and Bonwit and Cerise and Lathrop played HORSE. Julia Gillian was so used to playing MEERKAT with her parents, with her mother's unexpected shots and her father's predictable ones, that playing with her friends made it seem like an entirely different game.

"Controlling for variables doesn't work so well in an actual game," she observed, when the game was over and Cerise had won.

"Why not?" said Lathrop, who had never really gotten the concept of controlling for variables.

"Too many variables you can't control for," she said.

"Too many unexpected moves. Free throws are different."

"How many are you up to now?" said Cerise.

"One hundred forty-four."

"Still?"

"Still."

Free-throw practice had not been going well since she had begun controlling for Bigfoot variables. Every time Julia Gillian missed, she instinctively looked toward the lilac bush, where Bigfoot would ordinarily be lying down. Even when he had been asleep, his presence had been comforting to her. Now she had to look up to her apartment building, at her bedroom window, and imagine him lying on his long magenta pillow next to her bed. It wasn't the same.

"Free throws aren't everything," said Lathrop. "They're only one tiny part of a real basketball game."

"She's not going out for the basketball team, nitwit," said Cerise. "She's trying to become the World's Youngest Free-Throw Champion."

Cerise was being loyal, but Lathrop had a point. If you were going to control for variables you needed to control for everything possible. And it was nearly impossible to control for everything. Basketball, for example, included much more than free throws. Take dribbling, for example, a whole other skill that Julia Gillian had yet to master.

She kicked at the wood chips on the playground. All that time in the alley practicing her free throws, and she was still only up to 144. How in the world had that doctor in California made it all the way to 2,740?

"Ms. Gillian!"

Cerise and Lathrop and Bonwit turned to see who was speaking. Julia Gillian froze. She knew that voice. It was the voice of Ms. Caravaggio, her tall, basketball-playing, eighth-grade nemesis. And here she was, loping across the blacktop toward them, her frizzy blond hair floating behind her, dribbling a basketball.

"Ms. Gillian!" she called again.

She stopped in front of them and bounced the ball several times. It was obvious that Ms. Caravaggio was a pro. The basketball was like an extension of her long arm. She didn't even look at it when she bounced it. Was there anything in the world that she wasn't good at? Anything at all?

"What do you want?" said Julia Gillian.

Ms. Caravaggio stopped bouncing the basketball.

"I just wanted —"

"— what?"

Julia Gillian was surprised to hear how flat her own voice could sound. Was this really her, Julia

Gillian, talking back to the fearsome Ms. Caravaggio in this way?

Ms. Caravaggio frowned.

"I was going to ask if you wanted to play basketball with me," she said. "Forget it, though."

She bounced the basketball a few more times, still frowning.

"Why are you always so mean?" she said.

Suddenly Julia Gillian was angry. How could this  girl, who was good at everything, lived a perfect existence, and had never been sad a day in her life, possibly accuse her of being mean?

"You knocked me down!" said Julia Gillian. "You and all the other eighth-graders. You attacked me!"

"Yeah!" said Cerise and Lathrop together.

The attack-of-the-eighth-graders story had been told so often, Julia Gillian realized, that she herself had come to believe it. She had almost forgotten the real incident.

"We did not attack you, and you know it," said Ms. Caravaggio. "The door swung open, and it knocked you down."

Julia Gillian said nothing. This was, in fact, the truth of what had happened.

"And you didn't let us help you," continued

Ms. Caravaggio. "And you wouldn't talk to me in the alley. You won't even let me say hi to your dog."

"Why would she?" said Cerise. "Haven't you noticed how everyone's scared to use the third-floor bathroom?"

Ms. Caravaggio looked confused.

"Haven't you seen the line outside that tiny little gym bathroom every day?" continued Cerise.

"I have," volunteered Lathrop.

Julia Gillian stayed silent. Of course they had all seen the line outside the little gym bathroom. She herself had been part of that line on more than one occasion.

"And why do we all use that tiny bathroom?" said Cerise. "Because we're scared of you."

Oh no. Cerise was giving away their secrets.

"Scared of me?" said Ms. Caravaggio. *"Me?"*

"Not just you," said Cerise. "All the eighth-graders."

Ms. Caravaggio looked too surprised to speak.

"You're the Crazy Eights," said Bonwit. "You're all so tall. And loud. And —"

"Don't you think we were sixth-graders once, too? Don't you think everyone called us Sixlets? And then Sevvies? And now Crazy Eights?"

Ms. Caravaggio folded her arms across her chest and shook her head.

"In less than two years, you're going to be eighth-graders, too," she said. "Did you ever think of that?"

Julia Gillian looked at Bonwit and Cerise and Lathrop, who looked as surprised as she felt. Ms. Caravaggio was right. Julia Gillian would be a Crazy Eight before she knew it. She tried to picture herself tall and confident and loud, whipping dodgeballs around on the playground, careening up and down the dreaded eighth-grade stairs, fearlessly using the third-floor bathroom. Maybe the sixth-graders would seem small and puny to her when she was in eighth grade.

Ms. Caravaggio looked straight at Julia Gillian.

"You haven't been fair to me, Ms. Gillian," said Ms. Caravaggio. "Think about it."

Just then, Mr. Lamonte blew his whistle. Recess was over.

"Saved by the whistle," Cerise said dramatically as they ran to the door.

Once they were safely inside, Julia Gillian glanced back to see Ms. Caravaggio standing silent and tall, bouncing her basketball alone on the court, gazing after them.

That night at dinner, Julia Gillian told her parents that she was stuck at 144 free throws in a row.

"'Stuck?'" said her mother. "One hundred forty-four is great. I'm pretty sure that I could never in my life get up to 144."

Privately Julia Gillian agreed — her mother was far too interested in trying unusual shots to focus on free throws with the intensity that being a free-throw champion required — but she politely said nothing.

"I can't seem to get past 144, though," said Julia Gillian. "I'm controlling for all the free-throw variables I can think of, and I haven't made any progress lately."

The very thought tired her. Controlling for variables was difficult. From the floor where he lay next to her

chair, Bigfoot looked up. He swished his tail back and
forth on the floor. He yawned.

"You are a lazy dog," said Julia Gillian. "Lazy, lazy,
lazy. Aren't you, my lazy Bigfoot?"

He stretched out one paw, and then the other.
He yawned again. He rolled onto his side and stretched

all four legs. Julia Gillian admired the gold and white and brown of his fur. St. Bernards were noble dogs, and she had always been pleased that her own dog was a St. Bernard.

"At least I'm doing a good job controlling for Bigfoot variables," she said.

She was even keeping him safe from her parents, who weren't as careful as she was. Many mornings lately, she had woken to see her father standing in the doorway, holding Bigfoot's red leash in his hand.

"I'll take him out this morning," he would say.

"That's okay, Dad," Julia Gillian would say. "I don't mind."

It had turned into a bit of a challenge, keeping her parents inside in the early morning. The truth was,

Julia Gillian looked forward to taking Bigfoot out in the early morning. This had not always been the case. In the past, she had sometimes pretended to be asleep, so that her father or mother would take pity on their poor tired daughter, and take Bigfoot out for her. But no more.

It made her sad that Bigfoot was missing out on the doings of the neighborhood. The Bryant Hardware window had been decorated for Halloween, for example, and he hadn't even seen it. Now Mr. Bryant Senior and Mr. Bryant Junior were putting up the Thanksgiving decorations, and he would miss them as well.

"Your mother and I want to talk to you about that, sweetie," her father said now. "Don't you think Bigfoot misses his walks?"

Bigfoot looked up at Julia Gillian, and then at her father. He blinked.

"And his bat?" said her father.

At the word *bat*, Bigfoot looked toward Julia Gillian's room, where, up on the high shelf, his bat rested on top of the green book. Now he gave her father a hopeful look. Supposedly dogs understood very few words, but Julia Gillian had long suspected that this was not true. Look at Bigfoot. At the mention of his favorite things — bat, walk — he was fully awake and alert.

"Yes," said Julia Gillian.

Of course Bigfoot missed his walks and his bat. But that was not the point. The point was that variables needed to be controlled, and these were the variables that needed controlling if Bigfoot was to remain strong and healthy.

"And we're betting that you do, too, honey," said her father.

Julia Gillian remained silent. Of course she missed these things. The lump rose in her throat again. Didn't her father know that it wasn't easy, controlling for variables?

"Don't you think we should keep doing the things that make Bigfoot happy?"

The lump in her throat made it hard for Julia Gillian to talk, so she stayed quiet.

"Let's all go for a walk tomorrow," he said. "A long, slow walk."

CHAPTER EIGHTEEN

A Red Letter Day

When she woke up that Saturday, Julia Gillian looked out her bedroom window. It was early morning, and the fall leaves were beautiful in the sun. It was a perfect, late fall day. Maybe one long, slow walk wouldn't be too harmful. Bigfoot, down on his long magenta pillow, seemed to know that something special was in store.

"Come on, Bigfoot," said Julia Gillian. "Let's go for a walk."

He rose up from his pillow and stretched his front legs, then his back legs. At the door he turned and looked back at the high shelf of the bookcase. Julia Gillian knew exactly what was on his mind.

Do you promise not to shake that bat? she beamed telepathically to Bigfoot. He did not look at her, but he did wag his tail.

Okay then. I'll get it for you.

Bigfoot's jaws closed gently around his beloved bat. Julia Gillian shook her head. She still didn't understand

why Bigfoot loved that bat so much — the meerkat she had been trying to win was so much cuter — but love it he did. It had been several weeks since Julia Gillian started controlling for Bigfoot variables, and it was clear how happy he was to have the bat safely between his jaws once again.

All the way down the hall to the door of the apartment, Bigfoot's tail wagged back and forth happily, and he kept glancing up at Julia Gillian and her parents. Outside, her mother held the red leash, and they began to saunter down Emerson in the direction of 36th Street and Bryant Hardware.

"Hello," called a voice. "Good-bye."

They looked up to see Enzo leaning out the window and smiling. At the sight and sound of her, Bigfoot's tail wagged faster. Enzo held something up in the air, and Bigfoot stopped immediately.

"May he have a Bigfoot Wow?" called Enzo.

Most people would say *can* instead of *may*, but Enzo had known Julia Gillian's English teacher father for a long time, and they were both sticklers for proper grammar.

"He may," said Julia Gillian's father.

"Bigfoot Wow coming at you!"

Enzo tossed the Wow from the window, and Bigfoot dropped his bat and snapped it up.

Are you my good boy? Julia Gillian beamed telepathically to him.

You are my good boy, she answered telepathically.

Her parents had been right. It did feel good to be

outside walking on such a beautiful day, telepathically communicating with her dog. Bigfoot gulped down his Bigfoot Wow and picked up his bat again. He shook it gently back and forth between his jaws. Julia Gillian watched carefully. If he began to shake it violently, she was going to have to take it away from him. She had agreed to break the variables rules with this walk, but there were limits, and she would enforce them. Luckily, after a few back and forth shakes, Bigfoot settled into the rhythm of their walk. Julia Gillian's parents smiled at her.

"Take us on the exact long walk that you and Bigfoot would ordinarily take, honey," said her father.

"Yes," said her mother. "We don't want to miss any part of it."

Their eleven-square-block walks had long been Julia Gillian and Bigfoot's private after-school routine, but today she didn't mind sharing it with her parents.

"Bigfoot knows where to go," said Julia Gillian. "He'll show you the way."

As if he knew what she wanted, Bigfoot headed left at 36th Street, straight to Bryant Hardware, and stopped in front of the big display window full of Thanksgiving decorations. They were in luck because Mr. Bryant Senior was standing right there in the window, washing the interior of the glass. He saw them standing outside, and he climbed out of the window and joined them.

"Well, if it isn't Miss Gillian and her tiny dog. How are you?"

"Miss Gillian and her tiny dog are very well."

This was their routine.

"I haven't seen you in quite a while," said Mr. Bryant Senior. "Where have you been hiding?"

Julia Gillian didn't want to talk about Bigfoot's enlarged heart or controlling for variables, so she just smiled and said, "Around."

Then she turned to Bigfoot.

"Let's continue on," she said to Bigfoot, "shall we?"

They turned around and headed to Girard Avenue, where the kind person who lived at the house with the birch trees always kept a paw-print bowl filled with water out front, along with the laminated sign that read DOGS! PLEASE HELP YOURSELVES! Bigfoot helped himself, and Julia Gillian's parents admired the way he lapped the water without spilling any. He had always been a very neat dog. As usual, he drank all the water, but Julia Gillian knew that the kind person who lived there would refill it for the next dog who happened along.

"I wonder who lives here," said her father.

"A kind person who loves dogs, that's who," said her mother, which is exactly what Julia Gillian was thinking.

"Show them where we go now," she said to Bigfoot.

On to the bakery, where Zap worked part-time while he was finishing his chef studies at the Dunwoody

Culinary Institute. Julia Gillian was glad to see that he was there today, sliding giant cookies off a metal tray onto a cooling rack.

"Well hello, my Bigfoot," he said. "How are you today?"

Bigfoot's entire body quivered with his love for Zap. Next to Julia Gillian and her parents, he loved Enzo and Zap best in the whole world, with Bonwit close behind.

"Would you care for a Bigfoot Wow?" said Zap. "On the house."

Bigfoot had already had a Bigfoot Wow, but Julia Gillian felt it would be mean not to let him have another, especially since his beloved Zap was the one offering it to him.

"If you want one, you're going to have to drop your bat, you know," said Zap.

It was always hard for Bigfoot to drop his precious bat, but the lure of the Wow won out again, and he dipped his head and let the bat slide gently to the black-and-white-checked tile floor. Down went his second Wow of the walk. It was a red letter day for Bigfoot, thought Julia Gillian, and if truth be told, it felt the same way for her. It was so good to be taking a long walk with her dog.

At the doorway, Bigfoot turned, bat in mouth, to glance once more at Zap. Zap was waiting for Bigfoot's glance — it was their routine — and he did a little dance. Zap often made up little dances on the spur of the moment, and Julia Gillian knew that this

particular one was in honor of Bigfoot, who, of all the dogs who passed by the bakery, had long been his favorite.

Once outside, Bigfoot headed down Hennepin toward the Dunn Brothers coffee shop at 34th and Hennepin. To the right was the path to Lake Calhoun, and to the left was the way home. As if he knew that the variables were in effect, Bigfoot took a left.

"Do you think that dogs dream?" said Julia Gillian to her parents.

This was something she had always wondered, but never asked about.

"I don't know, honey," said her mother.

"Nor do I," said her father. "I'd like to know, but I suppose we never will."

Julia Gillian looked at Bigfoot, slowly making his way toward home on 34th Street. When he was younger and asleep, his legs had sometimes twitched and moved as if he was running. Julia Gillian used to watch him and imagine that in his dreams, he was racing through a forest with his dog friends. She pictured the forest as the kind that might have existed back when dinosaurs ruled the earth: enormous trees, canopies of leaves high overhead, and grasses and flowers of the kind that no longer existed. Bigfoot and his dream dog friends raced on, up and down the hills, through the forests and the river valleys, nothing to stop them.

At the end of their long walk, they drove to the Quang Vietnamese Restaurant for their traditional Saturday night dinner, including egg rolls and strawberry bubble tea. The kind Quang owners, who loved Bigfoot, allowed him to sleep under the booth while they ate. When they returned to their apartment building on Emerson Avenue, Julia Gillian and her parents and Bigfoot sat on the front stoop for a little while. It was such a

nice evening for November, much warmer than it usually was at this time of year, and some of the leaves still clung to the maple and oak trees on the block.

"So that was a typical Bigfoot–Julia Gillian long walk," said her mother.

"Indeed it was," said Julia Gillian.

When Julia Gillian was nine, the long walk had been nine square blocks. And when she was ten, it had been ten square blocks. They were up to eleven now, or they had been, until the controlling for Bigfoot variables began. But no matter what the parameters were, the long walk had always included Bryant Hardware, the kind Girard Avenue person's house, and the bakery where Zap worked.

Julia Gillian glanced up at Enzo and Zap's apartment. Maybe Enzo was choosing which book she would read tonight. Maybe Zap was practicing his juggling, or dreaming up a new recipe of his own creation.

"Are you a tired dog, Bigfoot?" said Julia Gillian.

She was sitting on the first step, and he was sitting on the sidewalk next to her. At the sound of her voice, he lay his head in her lap. That was the sign that he wanted to be petted behind his ears, and Julia Gillian was happy to oblige.

"Hello."

Julia Gillian looked up. A little girl stood on the sidewalk before them, with her parents hovering behind her. She was cradling a puppy in her arms. Julia Gillian knew this little girl. She was the same little girl who lived a few blocks away and had been scared to go to kindergarten a couple of years ago, because she didn't know how to tie her shoes. Although kindergarten had turned out fine — she had, of course, learned how to tie her shoes, and her teacher had helped her — Julia Gillian always thought of her with tenderness. And here she was, taller and skinnier, holding her puppy with great care.

"I have a new puppy," she said.

"I see that," said Julia Gillian. "What's his name?"

"It's a she," said the little girl. "We got her from the Humane Society. She's part husky and part border collie and part terrier and part who knows what. And I can't decide on a name yet. Right now I just call her Puppy."

Julia Gillian was surprised at such a stream of words from the little girl, who usually said no more than one or two

words at a time. She must be truly excited about her new puppy. Bigfoot raised his head and looked with interest at the puppy, sniffing the air around him.

"Have fun with Puppy," said Julia Gillian.

The girl's parents, hovering behind, smiled at Julia Gillian. They were grateful for the help she had been to their little girl, back in the kindergarten-fear days. The three of them, plus Puppy, moved off down the sidewalk. Julia Gillian watched them go. She and Bigfoot were the same age, so she had no memories of cradling him as a tiny puppy. For a moment she felt jealous.

Bigfoot yawned.

"Bigfoot needs his sleep," said Julia Gillian.

Tomorrow, she would go straight back to controlling for variables. Up the stairs they went. On Enzo and Zap's floor, Bigfoot paused and looked down the hall toward their apartment, then back at Julia Gillian.

"Sure," she said. "You can say good night to Enzo and Zap if you want."

Knock knock knock.

Julia Gillian didn't do her secret code knock on the door, because her parents were present, and she didn't want anyone but Enzo and Zap to be privy to the secret code. Footsteps came to the door, and she could tell by the lightness of the step that it was Enzo, and that she was barefoot. There was a pause. Julia Gillian knew that because she hadn't knocked their secret code knock, Enzo was looking through the security peephole. Enzo believed in safety and security, and she would never open the door unless she knew who was on the other side.

"Noodlie!" said Enzo, opening the door. "And Mrs. Gillian and Mr. Gillian! And Bigfoot."

"Bigfoot wanted to say good night," said Julia Gillian.

"Did you?" Enzo said to Bigfoot. She knelt down so that her face was on the same level as Bigfoot's.

"We took the long walk."

"Did you?"

"The eleven-square-block walk."

"Really?"

Enzo looked up at Julia Gillian and her parents. They all nodded. None of them mentioned the fact that an eleven-square-block walk meant that one of the Bigfoot variable rules had been broken.

"It must have been a happy day, then," said Enzo to Bigfoot.

He tilted his head and brushed his tail back and forth.

"Good night, Bigfoot," said Enzo. "Good night, Noodlie."

And they went upstairs to their own apartment. Once inside, Bigfoot went straight to the kitchen, laid his bat down beside his water bowl, and lapped up most of the water. As usual, he made no mess. Then he picked up his bat again and went to Julia Gillian's bedroom, where he lay down on his long magenta pillow and stretched luxuriously. She had always admired the way Bigfoot could lengthen himself out, as if every muscle in his body was in need of a good long stretch. She knelt down beside him and put her mouth next to his ear.

"Sweet dreams, my dog," she whispered. "Sweet, sweet dreams."

CHAPTER NINETEEN

Do You Dream?

The next morning Julia Gillian woke at dawn. She was not ordinarily an early riser, but sometimes it was pleasant to wake up early and lie in bed for a few minutes, looking out the window. In summer, she liked to climb out onto the fire escape outside her bedroom window in her pajamas and sit there, enjoying the early morning sun. Sometimes, in the summer, Mr. Hoffbeck, who lived in the apartment directly above, came out to water the flowers he grew in pots on his fire escape.

"Look out beloooooow!" Mr. Hoffbeck would call, and Julia Gillian would slide out of the way of the drops of water that splashed down when the pots overfilled.

In winter, Julia Gillian liked to curl up under her

quilts and look out the window. Sometimes snow
would fall, blanketing the bars of the fire escape in
white and muffling the noise of the city the way
that only snow could. Sometimes it would be so
cold that frost had formed on the inside of Julia Gillian's
window. On those days, Julia Gillian would coax

Bigfoot up onto the bed with her, so that she could scratch pictures into the frost with her fingernail and he could admire them.

Now it was November, which was neither fall nor winter. It was an in-between month, when you could always see your breath outside, and you needed to wear a jacket, but you could also see colorful leaves still clinging to the trees. Julia Gillian had always loved this time of year. She especially liked to press the toes of her shoes on the thin ice that formed on the mud puddles and watch the entire sheet of ice bend under the gentle pressure.

"Bigfoot," she said, aiming her voice in the direction of his long magenta pillow, which, ever since he was a puppy, had been next to her bed. "Are you ready to go out?"

No response. Bigfoot wasn't much of an early riser, either, which Julia Gillian generally appreciated. But it was Sunday, and she was ready to get up.

"Bigfoot, are you feeling lazy?"

She peeked over the end of her bed at the long magenta pillow. There he was, sound asleep. She reached down and tickled his right ear. This was a tried-and-true method of rousing Bigfoot. No response. Goodness, that long walk yesterday must have tired him out. She tickled his left ear. No response.

Julia Gillian had an odd feeling then. Everything seemed to slow down, including her heart. It was hard to move and hard to breathe. She eased herself out of bed and lay down next to Bigfoot, just as she had done last night. His bat was under his paw as always, and his eyes were closed. She laid her head against his side. His breath was light and quick, but when she stroked his ear again, he still didn't open his eyes.

"Mom? Dad?"

She could barely hear her own voice, but her parents materialized beside her as if they had flown down the hall from the kitchen. She heard her mother draw in her breath the way she did when she was startled or hurt, such as the time she had sliced her thumb open with the paring knife.

"Bigfoot's not breathing right," said Julia Gillian.

Her father's
ear was next
to Bigfoot's
nose.

"His eyes are closed," said Julia Gillian.

"We need to get him to Dr. Gowdy," said her father.

Her mother was already on the phone, dialing Dr. Gowdy's personal phone number, which she had given them in case of emergency. Julia Gillian could hear part of the conversation. *Breathing doesn't sound right. Eyes are closed. Won't get up. Yes, we'll bring him right in. Thank you.*

"Can you get up?" Julia Gillian whispered into Bigfoot's left ear.

He opened his eyes, blinked, then closed them again.

"I don't think he can get up," said Julia Gillian to her father.

"We'll carry him, then," he said.

It took all three of them — her father holding him around the middle, her mother cradling his hind legs, and Julia Gillian supporting his head — to carry him down the stairs and into the car. Julia Gillian could feel Bigfoot trying to help them; he tried to lift his head, and at one point he tensed his front paws as if he was trying to stand up. *Just relax,* she beamed to him telepathically. And he relaxed.

Dr. Gowdy was waiting for them. They went into the back examining room, the one next to the fountain. Julia Gillian kept her arms around Bigfoot the whole time that Dr. Gowdy was talking with her parents. *Slow and irregular heartbeat. Inability to move. Can put him in the vet hospital but it's only a matter of time.*

"It's your decision," said Dr. Gowdy at the end of the murmur of words.

That, Julia Gillian heard clearly. And she knew what it meant. Dr. Gowdy was telling them that they needed to decide if they were going to let Bigfoot die. She could sense her parents communicating silently above her head. She closed her eyes and pushed her face against Bigfoot's neck. He was still breathing quickly and lightly, the way he used to when he was younger and he would jump up and down in his happiness to see her. She was crying again.

"It's my fault," she said to her parents and Dr. Gowdy. "We shouldn't have taken him on that walk yesterday."

The three of them looked very sad. Dr. Gowdy was holding her mother's hand.

"It's no one's fault, Julia Gillian," said Dr. Gowdy. "Bigfoot is an old dog. This would have happened no matter what you or anyone did or didn't do."

She left them alone then, in the examining room. Julia Gillian looked up at her parents, and they looked back at her.

They could have talked, but they didn't.

They had already made their decision, and they all knew it.

Julia Gillian got right up on the table next to Bigfoot, and she lay down beside him, so that their faces were eye to eye. Was he hurting? Was her dog in pain? His soft fur was warm, and his breath tickled her nose. He opened

his eyes and looked into hers. She was so close to him that her gaze dissolved into his, and their eyes merged into one big brown dog-girl eye.

"Bigfoot?" she whispered. "Do you dream?"

He didn't blink. She began to sing very softly to him, a song with a melody that climbed up and down and went anywhere it wanted to go, which was what jazz was like. She sang about the Bryant Hardware window, and the DOGS! PLEASE HELP YOURSELVES! water bowl, and the bakery, and Bigfoot Wows, and how good it was to live right above Enzo and Zap. She sang about his skinny brown bat. Then she leaned back a little, put her hands on each side of his face and held his gaze.

"You have been the Dog of my Dreams," she whispered. "You will always be the Dog of my Dreams."

After a long time, Dr. Gowdy came back into the room. Julia Gillian and her mother and father all held Bigfoot and stroked his legs and his back and his neck while Dr. Gowdy gave him the injection. Julia Gillian laid her head on Bigfoot's side and felt his breath slowing.

It was all happening so fast.

It all happened so fast.

Now her heart started to hammer. She could feel it pounding in her chest and in her ears. At the same time, her mind slowed, and her own voice sounded inside her head. She was telling herself that Bigfoot had died. Then her parents were putting their arms around her, and all three of them were crying.

CHAPTER TWENTY

And Still We Choose to Love

Everything was too hard.

Everything was too hard.

Everything was —

— too hard.

The Sunday that Bigfoot died was a day unlike any that Julia Gillian had ever lived through. She and her parents sat on the living room couch together, holding hands. Julia Gillian had never felt such sadness. Her heart literally hurt with the pain of it. From the couch she could see Bigfoot's red leash hanging on its hook by the door. She knew that his food and water bowls were in the kitchen next to the pots and pans cupboard. His long magenta pillow lay next to her bed. His bat was in her lap.

"I never liked that bat," she said. "But Bigfoot did."

She started to cry again. Bigfoot had loved his bat, and she had loved Bigfoot, and if Bigfoot were here now he would be lying on the floor next to them all, with the bat tucked safely under his paw. He *should* be here, but he wasn't. This was so wrong that she couldn't even put it into words. Her parents were nodding, though. Maybe they felt the same way.

"We have to eat," said her father. "Don't we?"

Her mother nodded. It was Sunday night, and just last night they had been talking and laughing and eating at the Quang Vietnamese Restaurant. Bigfoot had been sleeping under their booth, and Julia Gillian had reached down to stroke his head.

"Let's order a pizza from Beek's," said her father.

Usually ordering a pizza from Beek's King of Pizza was a special treat for the Gillians, but not tonight. When the pizza came, none of them could eat more than a slice, even though it was their favorite, half pineapple with Canadian bacon, half sausage and mushroom.

"I have to call Bonwit," said Julia Gillian, and her parents nodded.

The conversation was very short. After she got the words out, Julia Gillian began to cry, and so did Bonwit, and neither of them could stop. They hung up without saying anything more, but that was okay, because they knew exactly how each other felt.

When it was time to go to bed, Julia Gillian put on her pajamas without looking at Bigfoot's long magenta pillow. She climbed up into bed without looking at it.

She pulled the covers up slightly over her eyes, so that if she happened to look down, she wouldn't see it. It had fit Bigfoot perfectly, and she knew that if she looked at it, she would still be able to see the indentations of his long body. Her parents stood in the doorway, watching her.

"Good night, sweet girl," said her mother.

"Good night, Daughter," said her father.

They crossed the room and bent down and kissed her. Then they turned out the light and closed the door

partway. But Julia Gillian, who was ordinarily a girl who fell asleep fast, lay awake. Even though she couldn't see it, the emptiness of the long magenta pillow filled her thoughts. She swung her legs out of bed and went into the living room, where her parents were sitting on the couch with their arms around each other.

"Can I go see Enzo?" she said.

Her father did not correct her bad grammar. Her mother did not point out how late it was.

"Of course," said her father.

"Of course," said her mother.

KNOCK. KNOCK. KNOCK.

KnockKnockKnock.

Knock. Knock. Knock.

There was the soft sound of bare feet on the floor, and then the door opened and Enzo held out her arms.

"Oh, Noodlie," she said. "My Noodlie. Your dad called me and told me."

She was crying, and Julia Gillian was crying again, and then she was sitting on Enzo's lap in Enzo's brown velvet chair. She was eleven years old, which was old to be sitting on someone's lap, but Enzo held her like a baby, and she did not resist.

"Enzo, do you believe that Bigfoot is in dog heaven now?"

Enzo tilted her head. Julia Gillian could tell that she was thinking hard.

"If Bigfoot is in dog heaven," said Enzo after a while, "what do you think he's doing?"

"Running. He's running with a pack of dog friends. Every dog in dog heaven is Bigfoot's friend."

Enzo nodded.

"He hasn't been able to run for a long time," said Julia Gillian, and she started to cry again. She had said *hasn't* as if Bigfoot was still alive.

"Will it ever get better, Enzo?"

Enzo cracked her knuckles. She did this when she was thinking deeply.

"You truly, truly loved Bigfoot," she said. "And loving something is a good thing."

"But it hurts so much."

Enzo closed her eyes and nodded. Julia Gillian noticed for the first time that she was holding Bigfoot's red leash in her hand. She must have taken it off the hook when she opened the door of her apartment, although she didn't remember doing so.

"That's what it means to be human, Noodlie," said Enzo. "It's the hardest, most beautiful thing about being human."

"What is?"

"That we love what is mortal," said Enzo.

"Was Bigfoot mortal?"

"Everything that is alive is mortal. And destined, someday, to die."

"Like Bigfoot."

"Like us," said Enzo, and she wrapped her arms tighter around Julia Gillian. "But love doesn't die. 'For thy sweet love remembered such wealth brings, that then I scorn to change my state with kings.'"

That must be a Shakespeare quote. Julia Gillian didn't know exactly what it meant. But it was about love, and she did know that all her life she had loved her dog, and she had loved him completely. She stayed on Enzo's lap until she felt sleepy. Then Enzo brought her back upstairs, and her parents tucked her in.

CHAPTER TWENTY-ONE

Glad for the Friends She Had

On Monday, Julia Gillian could not get out of bed. Her parents must have felt the same way, because they both called their schools and arranged for substitute teachers. It was a gray day, and the clouds hung low. Julia Gillian lay on the couch and pictured all her friends, going through the school day. Bonwit would be there, and he would tell them all. That was one tiny comfort, knowing that she wouldn't have to face her classmates without their knowing what had happened.

On Tuesday, she dragged herself to school. It was trumpet lesson day, and her trumpet felt heavy, as did her backpack. At the door she turned from force of habit to say good-bye to Bigfoot before she remembered the awfulness, which was the fact that there was no Bigfoot to say good-bye to.

"Come on, Daughter," said her father, when he saw her looking down the hall to where Bigfoot would ordinarily be, waving his tail.

"Okay, Father," said Julia Gillian.

Bonwit was waiting for her at the playground. He, too, was holding his trumpet as if it weighed much more than usual. He slumped under the weight of his backpack, which, as always, was filled with every textbook from every class. Bonwit was never unprepared.

"Hi, Julia Gillian," he said.

"Hi, Bonwit."

She could see on his face how sad he was for her. This was the good thing about a best friend; he knew how you were feeling. It was also not such a good thing, because Julia Gillian felt the urge to cry again, and she didn't want to cry in front of the entire school. Cerise and Lathrop, who were on the playground having a swinging competition, leaped off at the highest point of their swings. They brushed the dust from their jeans and came over to Julia Gillian and Bonwit.

"Hi," said Cerise.

"Yeah, hi," said Lathrop.

They both looked down at the wood chips of the playground. Julia Gillian could tell that they wanted to comfort her but didn't know what to say. Next to her, Bonwit leaned close so that he was speaking into her ear.

"I told them," he whispered.

Julia Gillian nodded. She was grateful to Bonwit.

"I'm really sorry, Julia Gillian," said Cerise, who looked as if she was about to cry.

"Yeah," said Lathrop, who *was* crying "Me, too."

This was a lot, coming from Lathrop, who never cried, and it was also quite something from Cerise, too, who was reserved that way. Julia Gillian stood on the playground hugging her trumpet to her chest. She was glad to have the friends that she had.

"We've got to finish the Reading Buddies project today," said Bonwit.

Julia Gillian knew that he was trying to change the subject, and she was grateful to him for that, too. Bonwit knew that her sadness over Bigfoot was so big that she couldn't talk about it, so he was offering her the Reading Buddies project to talk about instead.

Bonwit and Judith Montpelier, of course, were already finished with their Various and Sundry Nights of Fright project. Cerise and Mimi Frank were putting the final touches on theirs. Lathrop and his partner were behind, but that was not unexpected; Lathrop was a procrastinator who usually — although not always — came through in the end.

"How are you and Fergus coming along with yours, Julia Gillian?" said Cerise.

Everyone in the class knew of the travails Julia Gillian

had been through with her reading buddy. His steely eyes, his vertical hair, and his flatly stated dislike of virtually everything except dogs had been entertaining for everyone except Julia Gillian. It was only since they had begun writing and illustrating their own book about Tiny, the immortal St. Bernard, that Fergus had shown signs of life. Now the thought of seeing what new Tiny illustrations Fergus had made over the weekend — he was unstoppable when it came to drawing — deepened her sadness.

"We're coming along, I guess," she said.

The bell rang. The doors opened, and the students filed in. The teachers were standing in the hall outside their classrooms, as was the custom at Lake Harriet School. Bonwit and Julia Gillian walked in together,

Bonwit slightly ahead, as if he were trying to pave the way for Julia Gillian.

"I told some of the teachers," whispered Bonwit.

Mrs. K was standing by the lunchroom. At the sight of Julia Gillian, she took a step forward and raised her dog-head cane. They locked eyes. Mrs. K held the cane in the air as if she were saluting Julia Gillian, and then she stepped back against the wall. Julia Gillian felt her eyes pricking. All the important people, it seemed, knew what had happened to Bigfoot. Word had traveled fast.

Bonwit stuck close to Julia Gillian as they walked up the stairs to the landing where Mr. Mixler played the piano each morning and each afternoon. He was playing a song that they recognized immediately: "Song of My Soul," the very first song they had ever learned on the

trumpet, back in the beginning of fifth grade. But Mr.
Mixler was playing it differently this morning. He was
bent over the piano, both hands moving slowly over the
keys, as if "Song of My Soul" was an elegy, a song of
mourning. He looked up as Julia Gillian passed. Without

speaking, he held his
left hand out to her,
while his right hand
kept picking out the
melody. Julia Gillian
shook his hand
as she passed, and
he squeezed it
tight before he
let it go.

CHAPTER TWENTY-TWO

The Kindness of Strangers

At lunchtime, the line to the little gym bathroom was longer than ever. Despite the fact that she hadn't expected it would take over the entire sixth grade — she had just wanted to tell a good story — Julia Gillian was the one who had started the whole controlling for bathroom variables movement. And now look what had happened. Everyone was afraid to use the third-floor stairs. Everyone was afraid to use the eighth-grade bathrooms. Looking at the line, Julia Gillian felt a wave of impatience sweep through her.

It all seemed so silly.

Everything seemed silly now, compared with what had happened to Bigfoot. He was important. Losing him was the worst thing that had ever happened to her. Next to that, who cared about the eighth-graders and their scariness?

Julia Gillian opened her lunch bag and took out her tiny folded lunch note.

Be Brave

That was all the note said. Julia Gillian refolded it and slipped it back into her lunch bag. Then she stood up.

"Where are you going?" said Bonwit.

Julia Gillian nodded toward the long line at the gym bathroom. Bonwit squinted — it was possible that he needed glasses — and then nodded, as if he knew what she was going to do. Julia Gillian walked over to the line.

"Go ahead and use the third-floor bathroom," she said to them all.

Her friends and classmates looked at her, fear and confusion on their faces.

"Go ahead," she said again. "The eighth-graders aren't so bad. They'll leave you alone."

"Did they tell you that?"

"Yeah, did they tell you that?"

This was from a girl far back in line who looked as if she was in serious discomfort. Julia Gillian nodded.

"Yes," she said. "Indeed they did."

They hadn't promised, to be honest, but she was too tired to go into the whole story of how she had exaggerated the bathroom attack. There must have been something on her face, though, that reassured the sixth-graders in line, because several of them turned to one another and, as if they were communicating silently, turned en masse and headed for the third-floor stairs.

Ms. Caravaggio had been right. Julia Gillian had been unfair to her. Even though her life was perfect, and she had never experienced the kind of sadness that Julia Gillian was going through, there was no need to keep on with this silliness.

It was a long day, and a sad day, and yet when the final bell rang, Julia Gillian wished she could begin it all over again. She was relieved that the walk home was so long because she dreaded opening the door to her apartment.

"I don't want to go home," she said now to Bonwit.

"I don't blame you," said Bonwit.

They had reached the Intersection of Fear and were waiting for the little walking person to appear on the light. If Julia Gillian went home now, her parents would be there, which was out of the ordinary, because they usually stayed after school to finish their teaching work. But they didn't want her to come home alone today, without Bigfoot waiting for her, so they had told her that they would be there waiting for her. Bigfoot's stuffed brown bat would be there, but he would not. His water and food bowls would be in the kitchen, but there would be no water or food in them. His long magenta pillow would be beside her bed, but he would not be sleeping on it. She shivered.

"We can cross now," said Bonwit.

Julia Gillian nodded. The little walking person had appeared, and the cars were waiting. They crossed.

"Did you finish your reading buddy project?" said Bonwit.

"Not yet."

"But the Extravaganza's next week."

"We'll be finished by then."

This was a boring conversation — a question, an answer, a comment, another comment — but it was the only sort of conversation that Julia Gillian was capable of having right now. Bonwit knew this. That was because he was her best friend. It was good to have him, someone who knew exactly how she was feeling, walking beside her right now.

They passed Bryant Hardware, where Mr. Bryant Senior and Mr. Bryant Junior were putting the finishing touches on the Christmas decorations. They believed strongly that no Christmas decorations should ever be put up until the day after Thanksgiving at the very earliest, and Julia Gillian agreed with them. Seeing Christmas decorations at Halloween time, when it was still warm out, was discombobulating.

Tap. Tap. Tap.

That was Mr. Bryant Senior, tapping on the window to get their attention. He smiled down at Julia Gillian, and so did Mr. Bryant Junior. There was so much love in their smiles that Julia Gillian knew that they, too, had heard what happened. She didn't want to cry, but some tears leaked out anyway.

Bonwit and Julia Gillian did not part at Bryant Hardware, the way they usually did. Without talking about it, they kept on walking, past Gigi's Café, directly across the street from Our Kitchen, past Dupont and Fremont. They turned right onto Girard Avenue. This meant that they would have to pass the kind Girard Avenue person's house, and the laminated sign reading DOGS! PLEASE HELP YOURSELVES! next to the bowl of water by the birch tree.

Without saying anything, both Julia Gillian and Bonwit stopped by the birch tree. The bowl of water was low, the way it always was after Bigfoot had drunk his fill. Then the door to the house opened, and someone came down the steps carrying a jug of water.

No.

Could the jug-of-water-carrying person possibly be her?

It could. Julia Gillian and Bonwit stood staring. Ms. Caravaggio stood before them, holding the water jug, her head held high.

"You live here?" Bonwit said finally.

"Yup."

"*You're* the water bowl person?" said Julia Gillian. "You? Ms. Caravaggio?"

"Yup."

Julia Gillian was so surprised by this that her brain felt scrambled. All these years, Ms. Caravaggio had been the one filling the water bowl? This was Ms. Caravaggio's house? Ms. Caravaggio was the DOGS! PLEASE HELP YOURSELVES! person? Her thoughts were all jumbled up.

"Did you make that please-help-yourselves sign?" she said.

"Yup."

Ms. Caravaggio finished filling the water bowl and

stood up. She really was tall. Her cloud of hair was held back with a rubber band.

"Did you laminate it yourself?" said Julia Gillian.

"Yup."

A question, a yup. A question, a yup.

"So where's your dog?" said Ms. Caravaggio.

"He died," said Bonwit.

Ms. Caravaggio covered her mouth with her free hand. She set down her water jug with the other and started to cry. Julia Gillian's eyes filled with tears, and so did Bonwit's.

"But I've seen you with your dog for years," said Ms. Caravaggio to Julia Gillian. "You come by here every day."

Julia Gillian and Bonwit nodded.

"My dog died, too," said Ms. Caravaggio. "Three years ago. And I can't have another one because my grandma lives with us now and she's allergic. That's why I —"

She pointed to the water bowl and the water jug and the sign.

"You know," she finished.

Ms. Caravaggio was a dog lover, and dog lovers understood one another. Julia Gillian looked straight at Ms. Caravaggio.

"I'm very sorry," she said.

It was true. Julia Gillian was sorry about Ms. Caravaggio's dog, and she was sorry that she had been unfair to Ms. Caravaggio.

"My dog's real name was Bigfoot," Julia Gillian said then.

She didn't want to lie anymore. Ms. Caravaggio nodded as if she could tell what Julia Gillian was really trying to say.

"Bigfoot is a good name," she said. "My real name is Brunhilde."

"Brunhilde?" said Bonwit.

"Yes," said Ms. Caravaggio. "It's a secret. Now you know why I go by Ms. Caravaggio."

All three of them nodded. Without looking at him, Julia Gillian knew that she and Bonwit would keep Ms. Caravaggio's secret. Without saying anything, Bonwit and Julia Gillian turned and walked back to Bryant Hardware in silence.

"I guess she's not a dog hater," said Bonwit.

Julia Gillian shook her head.

"I thought she had the perfect life," she said. "I thought she had probably never been sad for a single minute."

Bonwit nodded. There was no need to say anything more. He knew what she was thinking, which was that Ms. Caravaggio had been terribly sad in her life, because she had lost her dog, too. She must have been as sad as Julia Gillian felt right now. And still she filled the water bowl for all the dogs who came walking by.

"Okay," said Bonwit.

"Okay," said Julia Gillian.

As always, Julia Gillian sensed Bonwit's telepathic thoughts. He knew that Julia Gillian felt bad about her treatment of Ms. Caravaggio, when, all these years, Ms. Caravaggio was the kind Girard Avenue person. And he knew how much Julia Gillian dreaded walking into her apartment without Bigfoot there to greet her. He knew that they had put off the inevitable by extending their walk home, but that now the time had come. Bonwit nodded at her. She knew that the nod meant *Courage*, and she nodded back.

CHAPTER TWENTY-THREE

Carried Along with the Tide

It was time for Reading Buddies, and Fergus Cannon was late. Julia Gillian got out their book and read through what they'd done so far. She had been happy with it before because it was such a cheerful story, but now she looked at it with new eyes. The girl in the story was the sixth-grade free-throw champion of the world. Her immortal dog, Tiny, was thirty years old and in perfect health.

Even though *The Cheerful Book* was a fictional story, these things didn't seem right anymore. Everything about the girl's life was happy. She never had any problems. As a result, the story was a little boring. This was hard to admit, but nevertheless, it was the truth. Take the fact that the girl had become free-throw champion of the world. Julia Gillian herself didn't care about being free-throw champion of the world anymore. After what had happened with Bigfoot, it seemed so unimportant.

And didn't everyone have problems, real problems? Including Ms. Caravaggio, who up until now had seemed to live a charmed life.

Julia Gillian was very tired. It had been a terrible thing to open the door to her apartment yesterday. Her parents were right there, waiting to greet her, but they all knew that nothing would be the same again. Now Fergus would be here at any moment, charging in with his hands full of new St. Bernard sketches. How would she get through this project with everything reminding her of Bigfoot?

She raised her hand.

"Yes?" said Mr. Lamonte.

"Mr. Lamonte, can I go get a drink of water?"

"I don't know, Julia Gillian. Can you?"

"May I go get a drink of water?" repeated Julia Gillian dully.

"You may."

Julia Gillian trudged to the door and out into the hall, which was quiet, the way it usually was when class was in session. There was noise from the stairway, though. She trudged in that direction.

The eighth-graders were returning from a field

trip, from the looks of it, pouring out of two yellow buses and streaming into the school. Practically running past the gym and the lunchroom and swarming up the steps, and then onto the eighth-grade stairs.

"Julia Gillian!"

She recognized that voice. It was Fergus Cannon's. But where was he?

"Julia Gillian!"

She caught a glimpse of him then, with his vertical hair and his striped shirt, right in the middle of the swarm of eighth-graders buzzing their way toward the eighth-grade stairs. He was waving a sheaf of drawings in the air and shouting her name. Then he was gone again, lost in the midst of the eighth-graders, swept away on the tide of tall loudness.

"Julia Gillian!"

His voice sounded fainter.

"Fergus!" she called. "Where are you?"

Then Julia Gillian heard a sudden shout, followed by generalized screeching from the direction of the stairs. The tide of eighth-graders on the stairs parted, and she was witness to the sight that Principal Smartt had warned them against for years: A small third-grader — not just any small third-grader, but Julia Gillian's third-grader — lay smushed on the second step from the top.

"Fergus!" yelled Julia Gillian.

All she saw, before the frizzy cloud of Ms. Caravaggio's hair blocked the way, was his sheaf of drawings. He was still waving them in the air.

At the sight of her reading buddy lying sprawled on the stairs, the eighth-graders milling about, and Ms. Caravaggio bending over him, Julia Gillian sprang into action. She was by Fergus's side in a moment, holding her arms out wide to protect him.

"Go away," Ms. Caravaggio ordered the other eighth-graders.

"I'm just trying to —" someone said.

"Go away," said Julia Gillian.

Julia Gillian and Ms. Caravaggio made shooing motions with their arms, and all the eighth-graders backed away. They receded up the stairs, and Fergus looked up at Julia Gillian.

"Thanks," he said.

"Are you smushed?" said Ms. Caravaggio.

"A little."

Ms. Caravaggio nodded briskly, as if a little smushing was not such a bad thing.

"Okay," said Ms. Caravaggio. "Julia Gillian will take care of you."

Then she was gone and Fergus was sitting up. Julia Gillian looked him over closely. His eyes were open. He was breathing. He was talking. There was no blood. No bones were poking through his striped shirt or his jeans. It did not seem as if an ambulance would be necessary. In fact, considering what he had just lived through, Fergus appeared to be in remarkably good shape.

"I heard what happened," said Fergus. "I'm so sorry."

Julia Gillian had been so focused on Fergus's possible injuries that she had forgotten, for an instant, about what had happened. Now it came rushing back through her. Her dog had died.

"I drew these for you," said Fergus, holding out a stack of drawings. "Can you tell who it is?"

He laid one on the stairs. There was Bigfoot as a puppy, sitting on his long magenta pillow, holding a red leash in his mouth.

"I tried to make him look like that photo you showed me," said Fergus. "Remember?"

Julia Gillian nodded. She did remember showing him the photo of Bigfoot, her favorite photo, the one she carried in the front pouch of her backpack. The likeness was remarkable. Even though he hadn't seemed to care, Fergus must have been paying attention. Now he spread all the drawings out on the stairs and waited silently for her to look at them.

"I used my imagination for the other ones," he said.

In one drawing, Bigfoot was standing in front of Bryant Hardware, looking at the window, which was filled with dog toys and treats. A tall girl with an oddly shaped head and very large feet — she looked a bit like a space alien — stood next to him, holding his leash. *Who's that?* Julia Gillian wondered, before she realized that the girl was meant to be her. Fergus was very good at drawing dogs, but not so good at drawing people. Maybe that was why he had drawn GILLIAN in tiny block letters on the back of the girl's shirt.

In the next drawing, Bigfoot lapped up water from a bowl in front of a tree.

In the next, he sat patiently, his paw extended to shake the hand of an unknown person holding out a bone-shaped treat.

In the next-to-last drawing, Bigfoot lay in the grass, his eyes open and a grin on his face. Above him, cloud-shaped bubbles held tiny images of dogs. Dogs running. Dogs swimming. Dogs playing.

And in the very last drawing, Bigfoot was on a cloud, looking down at the large-footed girl, who was standing

up, leaning against the railing of a fire escape. She was looking up at the cloud and holding a red leash.

"Do you know what that last one is?" said Fergus.

He was watching her closely.

"Me?" said Julia Gillian. "And Bigfoot?"

Fergus Cannon smiled in relief.

"Yes, it's you," he said. "And it's Bigfoot in dog heaven, looking down on you."

Julia Gillian's eyes filled with tears.

"He doesn't want you to be sad," said Fergus. "He wants you to be happy."

Julia Gillian nodded. She gathered up the drawings and stood up.

"Come on," she said. "We've got to finish our project."

On their way back down the hall to Mr. Lamonte's room, Julia Gillian was surprised to find herself putting her arm around Fergus Cannon's shoulder. This was not the sort of thing she usually did. It was a grown-up gesture, the sort of thing that Enzo or her parents would do to her. She gave him a little squeeze and then let go.

CHAPTER TWENTY-FOUR
The Way the Story Ends

The night of the Reading Buddy Extravaganza was cold and clear, typical for early December. Even though Julia Gillian could see the stars when she peered far up beyond the streetlamps, there was the feel of snow in the air. She and her parents and Enzo and Zap were wearing their winter jackets for the first time. Julia Gillian's arms poked out a bit beyond the sleeves, and she realized that she must have grown since last winter. It was an odd thing, growing. You couldn't feel it while it was happening, but when you returned to something after a long time — such as a winter jacket — it was a surprise to see that it no longer quite fit.

On the drive to school, Julia Gillian sat in back,

between Enzo and Zap. Her parents were in front, her mother driving with one hand on the wheel and the other hand holding her father's hand, which was the way she always drove. If Bigfoot were alive, he would have been in back with Julia Gillian. This was another hard thing to remember, and she was glad that Enzo and Zap were there to keep her company on the long backseat.

"What did you do for your reading buddy project, JG?" said Zap.

"You'll see," said Julia Gillian.

After a week of intensive work, she and Fergus Cannon had finally finished their project. Mr. Lamonte, who at last seemed to understand Julia Gillian's travails with her reading buddy, had kindly allowed them to come to school an hour early every day the week before the Extravaganza.

"Your project shows creativity and initiative," he had said. "I applaud your originality. Let's forge on through to the end, shall we?"

The lunchroom was brightly lit, with READING BUDDY EXTRAVAGANZA! posters hanging on the walls. Parents and children streamed in from all directions. Sixth-graders and their third-grade reading buddies were standing beside tri-fold Extravaganza projects. Most students had chosen to write a report about their book and illustrate it with paintings and sketches. A halo of shooting stars, constructed of glitter paper, hung suspended over Cerise and Mimi's project. Julia Gillian wasn't sure what the halo of shooting stars had to do with Amelia Earhart, but it was certainly eye-catching, and parents kept stopping to admire it.

Bonwit and Judith Montpelier's "Various and Sundry Nights of Fright" project had turned out beautifully. They had availed themselves of all Bonwit's mother's art supplies, and the paint colors they had chosen for their creature illustrations were glow-in-the-dark. For that reason, they had set up their project in the lunchroom supply closet, so that they could turn the closet light on and off to refresh the glowing colors. A taped-down trail of creature tracks invited passersby to enter the "Various and Sundry Nights of Fright" exhibit.

"Where's your project, Noodlie?" said Enzo.

"Over here," said Julia Gillian, nodding toward the table where Fergus Cannon stood.

She had to nod because she was holding her parents' hands. She was a sixth-grader, which was very old to be holding hands, but tonight Julia Gillian needed all the courage she could muster.

"Is that a brand-new papier-mâché mask?" said her mother, peering in the direction of the exhibit.

"Indeed it is," said Julia Gillian.

"Your reading buddy has interesting hair," said her father.

"Indeed he does."

The man standing next to Fergus Cannon must be his father, Julia Gillian realized. He, too, was short and skinny. His father's hair stuck straight up from his head, just as Fergus's did, and he was wearing the same kind of striped shirt that Fergus always wore. Julia Gillian's parents shook hands with Fergus's father, and Enzo and Zap introduced themselves.
Then they all stepped back to look at Julia Gillian and Fergus's project.

"Wow," said Enzo.

"Yeah," said Zap.

"Oh, sweetie," said Julia Gillian's mother.

Julia Gillian's father didn't say anything, but he cleared his throat several times. The mask *was* a good one, thought Julia Gillian, as she looked at it anew in the bright lights of the lunchroom. She had worked hard on it, putting all her knowledge of papier-mâché mask making into the construction of this particular mask.

"It looks so much like him," said her father.

"It does," said her mother.

Enzo and Zap just nodded. The mask did look like him,

thought Julia Gillian. It looked so much like Bigfoot that the lump rose again in her throat. She had managed to capture his noble profile, and the wise and gentle look in his eyes. Fergus had painted the mask when it was fully dry, and his excellent sense of color had shown itself, because the gold and brown and white were so close to the colors of Bigfoot's fur that Julia Gillian wanted to reach out and pet it. Her father cleared his throat again.

"Let's take a look at this story," he said.

"We wrote it ourselves," said Fergus.

"It changed a lot," said Julia Gillian.

"Yeah, it started out a lot different," said Fergus.

Do dogs dream?
That was the question that the girl had always wondered about. Sometimes her dog Tiny kicked his legs and grunted in his sleep, as if he were running. Tiny was the same age as the girl, and he had been her steadfast companion all her life.

"Your illustrations are wonderful, Fergus," said Julia Gillian's mother.

Many people, when complimented, tried to brush off the compliment or pretend that they were not worthy of it. Fergus, on the other hand, nodded matter-of-factly. He knew what he was good at.

Julia Gillian looked at Fergus with genuine affection. He had grown on her over the difficult course of their fall, and she realized that she would miss seeing him in Mr. Lamonte's room every week. She pictured him smushed on the stairs in the midst of the eighth-graders, still holding his sheaf of Bigfoot drawings high, and she mentally saluted him. This was a small third-grader with large courage.

Julia Gillian and Fergus looked out over the Extravaganza crowd. They had worked so hard on their story that they knew it practically by heart. They had made a good team, Julia Gillian as the writer, Fergus as the artist, both of them true dog lovers.

But Tiny was getting older. In fact, he was very old for a dog. He could no longer do many of the things that he used to do. The girl loved him even more the older he got and she wished that he would live forever. Every night before she went to sleep, she prayed that her dog would never die.

Enzo and Zap and Julia Gillian's parents and Fergus's father moved around the display, reading slowly and pausing to take in Fergus's artwork. Julia Gillian could tell that they liked the story. They might even have loved the story, because occasionally one of them would wipe her eyes or clear

his throat.

But the day came when Tiny did die. It was the saddest day of the girl's life, and she did not know how she would make it without her steadfast companion. She had loved her dog with all her heart, and now he was gone. Was this the hardest thing about being human?

Then she had a dream. She dreamed that Tiny was in another world. In this world, he was running through a forest. The trees were giant, and the flowers and grass grew everywhere. Snow capped mountains were in the distance, and lakes and rivers and creeks with pure, clean water.

Now Mr. Lamonte had joined the group. And here

was Mr. Mixler, silently reading the opening paragraph,

his baton making slow ovals through the air.

Tiny ran with his dog friends, on and on. Up and down the hills, through the forests and the river valleys. There was nothing to stop them, and they could run forever.

Mrs. K tapped her dog-head cane as she moved slowly around the table. She caught Julia Gillian's eye. She didn't wink this time, as was her habit, but she raised the dog-head cane slightly in the air and smiled.

Was this dog heaven? It made the girl happy to think of Tiny there, running on and on forever. She telepathically beamed her love to him, and through time and space, he telepathically beamed his love to her. Tiny was gone now, but he would always be the dog of her dreams. We had so many happy days together, thought the girl. So many, many happy days.

Mr. Mixler and Mrs. K and Mr. Lamonte were moving slowly around the display. Her parents and Enzo and Zap were standing before the papier-mâché mask of Bigfoot.

Julia Gillian joined them.

She pictured Bigfoot in her mind. She remembered the softness of his fur, especially behind his ears, and the way he stretched himself out on his long magenta pillow. She thought about his patience and gallantry, and how devoted they had always been to each other.

Julia Gillian looked out over the Reading Buddy Extravaganza crowd. All her friends were here, and her friends' parents, and her teachers. She was surrounded by people who had known her all her life, people who loved her. *The hardest thing about being human*, Enzo had said, *is that we love what is mortal.* Julia Gillian looked around the crowd. Everyone here was mortal. Bigfoot had been mortal. She herself was mortal.

Was Bigfoot in dog heaven now? She pictured him running with his dog companions, free and happy. She pictured him looking down from a cloud in the sky, watching over her as she went about her days. Right at that moment, there in the Lake Harriet lunchroom surrounded by her friends and family, love for her dog swept through her. How happy she was that he had been hers, and she had been his. Enzo was right. It was hard to be human and to love what was mortal. But it was beautiful, too.

This book was designed and art directed by Marijka Kostiw.
The jacket art and black-and-white interior illustrations were created digitally by Drazen Kozjan.
The display type was set in Mrs. Eaves Smart Lig, which is a font created in 1996
by Zuzana Licko, a font designer and cofounder of the Emigre type foundry.
Mrs. Eaves is based on the font Baskerville and named after Sarah Eaves, who became
Baskerville's wife and finished printing the volumes he left incomplete on his death.
The display was also set in F 2 F Madzine, a font designed in 1994 and 2003 by font designer
Alexander Branczyk, who is a partner of Frankfurt design company Xplicit.
The text type was set in 14-pt Adobe Garamond Pro, which was designed in 1989 by font designer
Robert Slimbach for Adobe, and is based on type designs of sixteenth-century printer Claude Garamond.
This book was printed at R. R. Donnelley & Sons Co. and production was supervised by Jess White.